THE VAMPIRE OF SIAM
A DARK CHRISTMAS

JIM NEWPORT

Encyclopocalypse Publications
www.encyclopocalypse.com

A DARK CHRISTMAS

THE VAMPIRE OF SIAM, BOOK 5

JIM NEWPORT

BOOKS BY JIM NEWPORT

The Vampire of Siam

Ramonne: The Return of The Vampire of Siam

The Reckoning: A Tale of The Vampire of Siam

Chasing Jimi

Tinsel Town

The Siamese Connection

A Dark Christmas

PRAISE FOR JIM NEWPORT

THE VAMPIRE OF SIAM

"Grand Guignol entertainment…good for nibbling on the beach."

— JAMES ECKARDT, THE NATION.

"Chilling and morbidly hilarious. Newport's intimate knowledge of the Far East makes this an ultra-realistic journey into terror."

— PULITZER PRIZE NOMINATED AUTHOR CHRIS BUNCH.

"Well-researched, engrossing, smart and sexy. A grave-yard smash."

— BOBBY 'BORIS' PICKETT, SINGER-SONGWRITER: THE MONSTER MASH.

Rating: 5 stars

— JOHN WALSH, MANGO SAUCE.

RAMONNE

"Newport retains, from his first novel, a sharp sense of place for modern Bangkok. This is the trendy Bangkok of the Emporium Suites, the skytrain, the Q Bar, the Bed Supperclub."

— THE NATION.

"Newport artfully adapts the vampire legend into a Mekong cocktail of surprises."

— CHRISTOPHER G. MOORE.

THE RECKONING

"Newport's novels succeed in their purpose: they entertain."

— THE NATION.

"The books are rich in cinematic imagery...and fascinating details of Thai history."

— THAILAND TATLER.

CHASING JIMI

"Did you miss the 1960s? This funny yet loving and respectful adventure mystery will take you back."

— JERRY HOPKINS, AUTHOR OF THE DOORS: NO ONE HERE GETS OUT ALIVE.

"Newport has gone from the vault of the dead to the electrifying life of Jimi Hendrix. If you can remember Woodstock, you will enjoy this book."

— *LANG REID, PATTAYA MAIL.*

TINSEL TOWN

"It moves like a runaway asteroid."

— *TIM HALLINAN, BESTSELLING AUTHOR OF THE POKE RAFFERTY SERIES (SET IN BANGKOK).*

"Tinsel Town is the best introduction-to-Hollywood novel I've ever read."

— *DAVID GILER, PRODUCER/WRITER OF THE FILMS ALIEN, UNDISPUTED, MYRA BRECKINRIDGE AND MANY MORE.*

THE SIAMESE CONNECTION

"Jim Newport is a writer with great skills. Non-stop, hold your breath action. A true thriller. "

— *LANG REID, PATTAYA MAIL*

"Newport clearly knows Bangkok…An easy read."

— *BERNARD TRINK, BANGKOK POST.*

The Vampire of Siam

A Dark Christmas

INTRODUCTION

Dear reader,

It's been almost twenty years since I wrote The Vampire of Siam. At the time, I had no idea it would spawn four sequels.

My career was (and still is, occasionally) as an Emmy nominated production designer. I've designed over 100 feature films and television series. Brokedown Palace, The Piano Lesson, The Shield, Bangkok Dangerous, and "Lost" are a few of my credits.

Therefore, when I started writing—about thirty years ago— it was screenplays that I tried my hand at. I wrote a lot of them. I even made some money. Nothing was ever produced, but that's the strange thing about screenwriting—things get optioned or bought (you get paid) and then they sit on the shelf.

By the early 90s I had decided I wanted to live in Thailand —Phuket in particular. I had found the perfect little house and I kept my bags there, and whenever I could, I returned. I became known and started to get film work there (Men of War was the first, Mechanic Resurrection was the last).

One evening, I was sitting in the outdoor beer garden on the roof of the old Tower Inn on Silom Road with a friend, when the brand new skytrain turned the corner headed for Chong Nongsi station. I had just bought a mini VCR camera, and I reflexively aimed it at the train. As it went by, I did a slow pan down below the tracks—using the night vision filter. I expected to see construction, but instead I saw a graveyard! A huge cemetery, occupying an entire city block. A high wall ran around the perimeter, which is why I'd never seen it before.

I thought to myself "…now that's a home for a vampire!"—and the vampire of Siam was born.

The next day I visited the marvelous Chinese-Portuguese graveyard. Prominent in that night vision film, the Xavier Mausoleum was hauntingly beautiful, and has had a part to play in all four books so far. Today there are only a few small sections of the Chinese cemetery left next to the Tower Inn, and another along Narathiwat Road. The land holding those graves is worth well over a million baht per square wa (four square meters).

I made my first trip to Cambodia in 2001, when it was still recovering from the Khmer Rouge regime and massacre. I went to Angkor with two old Asia hands and we actually spent a night atop the temple, and wandering the grounds.

I decided very quickly that my vampire was of French descent, and he came to Southeast Asia on Henri Mouhot's historic voyage that uncovered the ancient ruins of Angkor. I subconsciously named him Ramonne Delacroix—Ramonne of the Cross.

Assuming the vampire would be the antagonist of the piece, I invented Martin Larue—devil-may-care American playboy who made Bangkok his playground—as the protagonist. Newly divorced in 2001, I explored Bangkok's sordid dark side—the Eden Club, etcetera. I decided that a vampire (and Martin) living in Bangkok would be familiar with such places, so I changed the names and added them to the mix.

The story was so much fun to tell, and the two lead characters so endearing, that when it was finished, I found myself in mourning. I had killed Ramonne!

And so I did what every writer of every successful vampire movie (or book) does—I brought Ramonne back to life and happily propelled him and Martin through three more adventures.

The city of Bangkok has changed—almost beyond recognition—from the time I first arrived in 1987. Then, there were no meter cabs. You had your Thai girlfriend wave one down and negotiate the fare while you hid in the bushes (yes, there were bushes in Bangkok then).

There was no crowded knock-off market in the middle of Patpong. There were bars with tables outside and large-screen TVs showing spaghetti westerns and Pink Panther films.

There was no skytrain, so the average Thai had no idea there was a Royal Bangkok Sports Club with a golf course and horse race track right across from the Erawan Shrine.

Lately, the rapidity of the change is unnerving. The complete disregard for Bangkok's history, and the obliteration of the skyline with one massive skyscraper after another, has taken its toll on the health of the population. I get up from Phuket every couple months and return with a persistent cough and a sore throat for the next two weeks. I doubt wearing a paper mask is the solution to this enormous problem.

But it's not just dust that this race to the skies showers on the city's pedestrian population. Contractors wantonly ignore construction codes and orders—inevitably causing injuries and death. When this happens, local officials are difficult to corner for comment, while the contractors scramble for "fall guys" to sacrifice.

More often than not, the managing director or owners of the project are never pursued for any compensation or legal recourse. Generally, the countless victims of these tragedies— the unlicensed foreign workers (Burmese, Cambodian) and their families—are quickly bought off for a pittance.

A dear friend of mine's family were victims of just such a travesty several years ago, and I watched in anger as he fought for not just compensation for the loss of his son, but for an admission of guilt. He was no novice in the ways of the Land of Smiles, but he was stifled at every turn by a legal system that favored the corrupt and powerful.

Hence, I've taken liberties to tell a version of his tale, not just because he and his family suffered so much, but so that their story and hundreds of others are not forgotten.

Jim Newport
Phuket, Thailand
2020

*My heartfelt thanks to my dear friend
Patrick "Shrimp" Gauvain and his family
for allowing me to portray a fictionalized
version of the loss of their beloved son Leo*

1
———

November

Jenga building blocks.

It took Martin a moment to remember the name of the game played by bargirls in the thousands of bar beers throughout the kingdom. The girl and her customer take turns removing one block at a time from a tower constructed of fifty-four wooden blocks. Each block is then placed on top of the tower, creating a progressively taller and unstable structure. The game ends when the tower falls. The winner is the last person to successfully remove and place a block.

The three hundred and fourteen-meter tall skyscraper he faced looked like it had been designed during a Jenga competition. The luxurious MahaNakhon Tower, Bangkok's tallest structure, has two unusual cuboid-surfaced spirals cut into its side and top, giving it an unnerving, unsafe appearance.

Martin Larue was on the second level of the Chong Nonsi skytrain station. On each side of him were his children—eighteen-year-old adopted son Hon, and eight-year-old daughter Nina.

It was early afternoon and already the giant Christmas tree

standing in the courtyard of the MahaNakhon Plaza was fully illuminated. Barely mid-November and yet the holiday decorations were everywhere. The day after Halloween, the goblins and ghouls come down and the twinkle lights and candy canes go up. Thailand is a Buddhist country, but you wouldn't know it at this time of year.

Holding little Nina's hand, Martin led them to the northern end of the platform and down the stairs to the main road alongside the Chong Nonsi Canal. Martin's driver could have fought the ever-present traffic jams and brought them here in leather-cushioned comfort, but Nina enjoyed the raucous crowds and chaotic energy of the skytrain, and so Martin found himself joining the hoi polloi more and more, and had to admit that there was no better way to travel around the sprawling megalopolis than on its ever-expanding network of skytrains and subway lines.

They walked north to Silom Road. The construction cranes and earth movers were busy as usual, turning whatever recognizable landmarks were left in the ancient city into indistinguishable steel, glass, and concrete blocks. For every architectural marvel like the MahaNakhon Tower there were scores of unremarkable, bland, vapid housing and commercial projects.

Walking in the shade afforded by the skytrain's massive pedestal and rail network, they passed an old stone wall incongruously covered with graffiti. Graffiti was a rather recent nuisance in Bangkok, the Thai people had always seemed too polite for such an irreverent act.

The wall ended and the seven-story Silom Plaza began. Just before the plaza was a paved narrow driveway. Martin led them into the narrow alley, passing a row of massive air-conditioning ducts blasting hot humid air. Eventually they were behind the shopping plaza and the paved alley came to an end. An ancient stone wall framed what appeared to be a very small park.

A footpath led to an opening in the wall. Martin led the way and they followed the path, past stately ficus trees shading a neatly manicured lawn. The silence and serenity they experienced was as if they had stepped back in time. They were surrounded on all sides by the skyline of the massive modern city while they strolled through a country park.

Except it wasn't a park.

It was a cemetery. An ancient graveyard.

Or rather, what was left of one. A few headstones and a couple of plaques dotted the neatly-kept yard. A large stone mausoleum stood in the center of the park. The name "Hernando" was carved in the granite over the entry.

This was all that was left of the once massive Chinese-Portuguese Hernando Cemetery. For hundreds of years it had contained and preserved the remains of intrepid souls who had voyaged unfathomable distances to explore and inhabit this remote Asian seaport. Generations of families buried their ancestors in old-world splendor in what was the very heart of the city.

By the 1950s it was witness to the adjoining Silom Road's change from a dirt road to a paved street. By the next decade the rice paddies of the Patpong family were being turned into bars and brothels for American soldiers on "R and R."

Once the skytrain made its inevitable first pass around the cemetery in 1999, the site was doomed. It stood its ground valiantly for another ten years, but the laborious removal of the inhabitants began in earnest in 2010, and by 2015 the earth movers and wrecking crews came and slowly transformed the graveyard into every Bangkok developer's dream—a construction site.

The mausoleum stood alone now—a backhoe parked on one side, a wrecking ball on the other.

"Why are we here?" Hon asked plaintively.

"Because it will soon be gone," Martin replied.

"What will be gone?"

Martin motioned to the mausoleum. "This...It has stood

here for centuries. It honors a man who died in 1872. Then, in the second half of the twentieth century, it was frequented by Ramonne Delacroix—a man who died in 1860."

"That's ridiculous," Hon snorted.

Martin smiled. He realized that Hon had no memory of his own encounter with the vampire in the Temple of Bayon at Angkor. He was just five at the time, and the vampire had abducted him to use in a battle with Zhoupeng, the thousand-year-old, all-powerful vampire who had been the one to "turn" Ramonne at Angkor one hundred and sixty plus years ago. Ramonne needed the power of the child's innocence. It took Martin a long time to forgive him for that transgression.

"Within the next week, this final bastion of a long-gone era will finally fall to the wrecker's ball."

"And what does this have to do with us?"

"It has everything to do with us. It was here that my destiny was changed forever by a chance encounter. That encounter led me to meet your mother. And that encounter almost got me, you, and your mother killed—more than once. It was here that Nina was nearly sacrificed before she was born, and it was here that the subject of that first encounter—the un-dead Ramonne Delacroix—sacrificed himself to save her."

Nina was not listening. She was more interested in a tiny lizard that she was cajoling with pieces of a granola bar.

"Seriously...? That is such bull," Hon retorted.

"No. No it's not. Sit down, son."

Martin took a deep breath and then began the story he had been waiting so many years to tell his son.

"Twenty years ago, I was a wealthy bachelor who settled in Bangkok when I inherited my father's publishing empire. I chose not to be involved in the day-to-day business, but rather to dabble in cinema journalism. But Prakasan, my editor at the *Bangkok Times*, thought I needed some excitement. He sent me out with the police on a ride-along. My guide was Lieutenant Colonel Boonsong. I unwittingly accompanied the police to a murder scene—here at Hernando Cemetery. They locked me in the back of a police car. You know...the kind with no door handles. But I was clever, and before I was discovered, I glimpsed the body of a girl with dyed hair sprawled naked across the cold stone bier in the center of the tomb.

"I did some research and found a trail of lost souls whose bodies seemed to end up in the Chao Phraya River, or as victims of random hit-and-runs. I convinced Prakasan I had uncovered a serial killer in the City of Angels. The article was front-page news and led to a visit from the murderer himself—a hundred and seventy-seven year-old French vampire."

"Ramonne Delacroix," offered Hon.

"Yes. Sophisticated, worldly, charming, and dangerous, Ramonne was at first determined to kill me. But it seems, in me, he found a kindred spirit. An unlikely bond was formed as I became intoxicated by the vampire's power to reveal the past glories of Siam and Angkor Wat that he had witnessed. He divulged that he had been paying off Boonsong to carry on his bloodsucking activities without interruption. I agreed to transfer my wealth to the vampire for the privilege of following him on his binges in Bangkok."

"Sex and death...those kind of binges?"

"I quickly drew the line at the death part...but the sex *was* amazing."

"I really don't want to know."

"Hon, it was a long time ago, and I was a bachelor."

Hon sat with his arms crossed. "Go on."

"Eventually my article forced Boonsong to confront the vampire, and insist that he no longer operate in Bangkok. This infuriated Ramonne, who swore vengeance. I followed him to the opening of a huge nightclub. Ramonne had been stalking the owner's girlfriend—the sexy young socialite Areeya 'Yaya' Boonsong, the colonel's daughter. In a fiery shootout, he kidnapped her."

"Mom?"

"Yes...Mom. In a ransom note, Ramonne demanded a meeting with Boonsong—alone—at Wat Arun, the Temple of Dawn. Of course, the colonel didn't come alone, and a dozen elite police battled the vampire on the 200-foot tower on the banks of the Chao Phraya. Ultimately they suffered defeat, and Ramonne dispatched Boonsong to hell with great pleasure. I had been watching, and entered the arena wielding a shotgun. This was potentially an instrument of destruction for the vampire, for if he was decapitated on hallowed ground—Wat Arun is indeed hallowed ground—his body would incinerate with the rise of the sun."

"You've been watching too many movies."

"This was *not* a movie. I knew that what I was trying to do would be futile. But I had to try. To save Areeya. But then he let me know that she was in no danger. He smiled and suddenly he compelled me—*willed* me—to pull the trigger.

"The next day, following instructions left by the vampire, Areeya and I went to his hidden lair. Here, amongst unbelievable treasures, was a note that told of his weariness...'with the changing world, and with the hunt.' He left several bank accounts for me to manage as I saw fit. Obviously he had no need of my money.

"I learned a lesson in the preciousness of life's every moment—*from a vampire.*"

Hon still had his arms crossed, but had leaned back against the wall, and was looking askance at Martin. "You said that Mom was pregnant with Nina, and that they were both nearly sacrificed here...but that the vampire saved them...How? You just said you killed him."

"And *that* is another story." Martin smiled.

The sun was beginning to wane when they finally left. Nina was asleep and in Martin's arms. He turned at the wall and gazed back at the mausoleum one last time.

Martin's responsibility to the École Des Orphelins d'Angkor—the orphanage in Siem Reap, Cambodia that he founded—went beyond merely financial. He started the orphanage in 2004, with sixteen children—Hon included—rescued from a life scavenging through a mountain of garbage outside of Phnom Penh. He and Areeya personally hired the staff, and when Areeya became pregnant, they returned to Bangkok with adopted Hon. They left the school in the competent hands of Justin and Julianne, a couple of archaeology students who came to Cambodia to work with the Angkor Conservancy. Martin assured them they would return, and they did—a year after the birth of their daughter.

Martin loved being a father.

He loved his children.

Little Nina Simone Larue was the apple of his eye. He adored her. He doted over her. She was a beautiful girl. A wonderful child. It had taken so long...two years of IVF injections and false hopes. When she was finally born on New Year's Eve, it was truly a miracle.

But Hon—his handsome boy—was unique.

He had always been a good student, getting A-grades in most subjects at Shrewsbury International School. But it wasn't until the family returned to Siem Reap that Hon truly began to shine. It was here that Hon saw his first piano. The orphanage had acquired the Steinway as a gift from the InterContinental Hotel when it went through a major renovation in 2008.

It's unknown what it was the boy played when he sat down that first time. It wasn't Bach or Beethoven...in fact, it's not known if it was an existing piece of music. But it was magical. All who heard it were transfixed.

The boy had a natural understanding of the keyboard, and an innate relationship with the instrument. In the coming months he progressed rapidly. Martin hired the closest thing to a tutor, Pierre, an eccentric French classical pianist residing in

Cambodia for unknown reasons. He was immediately in awe of little Hon's command of the instrument.

He told Martin that Hon was that very rare person. He was a prodigy. A musical genius.

He told Martin, "Piano talent usually expresses itself as an ability to take the myriad problems in a piano piece and somehow simply unite them and make music out of it, rather than a series of stumbles and fumbles. Prodigies don't care about mistakes, they are too far into the music. *That* is your son."

Within a year it was evident to Martin that they had outgrown Siam Reap. In the shadow of the temples of ancient Angkor, the little hamlet served mainly as a support mechanism for the massive tourist traffic. A sophisticated urban center it was not.

Their son was rapidly exhibiting a skill that they needed to return to Bangkok in order to pursue.

So once again they found themselves in the big city. Martin enrolled Hon in the Harrow International School for The Arts. The boy was not shy; in fact, quite the opposite. The piano had given him a new identity, and he took to it. He possessed that persona. Within two years he was known simply as "the Pianist."

The boy basically skipped the normal route of schooling— grade school to junior high, etcetera. His genius had been recognized and celebrated so much that Martin chose to "home school" him at an incredibly high level. He brought the best of the best scholars on each curricular level into his home, allowing Hon to pursue his musical career unabated.

The boy soon outgrew Bangkok.

At the age of twelve, Hon was a sophomore in high school, and by fifteen he had graduated and received a full scholarship to the Royal Academy of Music in London.

Concerts soon followed. Within seven months he was performing regularly in Europe, while continuing his studies. In two years he had completed the undergraduate course at the Royal Academy and been signed by the William Morris Agency as a solo performer. He gave his last performance as a student at Carnegie Hall.

By the time he returned to Bangkok during the school summer vacation, Areeya hardly recognized him when they met outside immigration at Suvarnahbumi Airport on the eve of Hon's eighteenth birthday.

They celebrated with a private performance for family and friends in the Author's Lounge of the Mandarin Oriental. The family—Areeya, Nina, Areeya's mother Rose, her cousins, her aunts, her cousin's cousins, her aunt's cousins, Martin's most intimate friends, as well as the few teenage friends that Hon had accumulated in the international arena that had been his upbringing—were all gathered to hear him play.

He was definitely a handsome boy. His longish hair curled over his ears and turned up at the nape of his neck. He wore bangs, as was the millennial retro style, and Martin thought it suited his sweet mysterious persona perfectly.

At Hon's request, a small rhythm section had been assembled. Hon didn't know them but he knew *of* them. And he knew what he wanted to play.

As birthday parties went, it was fairly unusual. It seemed more of a celebration for the adults than for the child crossing into adulthood. No one thought of Hon as a child. His musical skills had given him the posture of an adult long ago.

Hon chatted casually with the musicians as people took their seats. Then he sat at the Steinway. He nodded to the drummer and they began Dave Brubeck's "Take Five."

That was six months ago. Since then Hon had performed with Yo-Yo Ma and Wynton Marsalis at Lincoln Center, and had done a sixteen-city tour of Europe with Diana Krall.

His agents signed him with Blue Note, with the first sessions scheduled in January in Cologne, Germany. At his parent's encouraging, he took a four-week break to be with them through the holidays. But he insisted that the trio he would record with be flown to Bangkok so they could rehearse.

He returned home to Bangkok shortly after Thanksgiving to the delight of his doting parents.

————

Martin was glad he had chosen to finally tell Hon the "family secret." He was certain that Hon still thought he was making up the whole fantastic tale, but at least he now knew—his dad was once a vampire's friend and confidante.

A great burden was off his shoulders.

"Feeling smug are we?" Areeya sat down opposite Martin in the enclosed patio that faced Lumpini Park and the setting sun.

"I don't what you mean."

"I know that look."

"I suppose you're right. We've two beautiful children—"

"One a prodigy."

"Yes. True. But give Nina chance...she's only six."

"But that's not what you're gloating over."

"Oh?"

Areeya crossed her arms and cocked an eyebrow. "You *told* him."

Martin crossed *his* arms. "Told him *what*?"

"You told him about *him*."

"Who did I tell about who?"

"Oh, for God's sake, Martin. He told me...He thinks you're insane."

Martin put down the book he originally had intended to read. "It was time. He needs to know."

"Why? That's all over. The past is the past."

Martin smiled. One of a Thai woman's most enduring qualities is her ability to forgive and forget—personified by the expression, 'The past is the past.'

"Yes, that's true. He's gone. But he gave his life for us...for you...for Nina. And before that, he did the same for me."

"He also abducted me and killed my father."

"Your *corrupt* and murderous father."

"True, but he also abducted Hon as a baby and played Russian roulette with him and the Lord of Darkness."

"And he won."

Areeya uncrossed her arms and leaned back on the sofa.

"Martin...He's gone. It's been nine years. We're *normal* people, finally. Why did you have to tell Hon now?"

"Because he needs to know. We know this world is not what others think it is...and he needs to know that, too."

"Are you expecting to meet another vampire? Are you expecting Hon to meet a vampire?"

Martin stood and walked to the window. As the sun was sinking, it gave off the orange glow that caused some to call Bangkok the "Big Mango."

"No, I don't expect to encounter another vampire. But Hon? He's embarking on a life as a world-touring musician. I think its information he needs."

Areeya got up and stood next to Martin. A long moment passed before either of them spoke. Martin took her hand. "It's who we are. He needs to know that, too."

Areeya put her arms around him. "I know...but he still thinks you're insane."

2

The vampire stretched. It felt good. He'd had a good sleep. The Toyota Granvia van had been stripped of its rear seats to provide room for the elaborate teak coffin. Ramonne Delacroix had hardly noticed the 800-kilometer journey. He ascertained that night had indeed fallen, and climbed out of his coffin.

The interior of the luxurious vehicle was more like a private jet than a limo, and Ramonne availed himself of the specially stocked bar and its bottles of Bordeaux. He chose a 1999 Château Ferrière Margaux and relaxed in the deep leather lounge chair.

The vehicle had crossed over the Sarasin Bridge and sailed through the sleepy island checkpoint without stopping, and was now traveling parallel to the moonlit sea.

Phuket was one of the places in Thailand that Ramonne had heard of but never paid much attention to. Currently, corruption and environmental decay made the headlines. But there had been times—the halcyon days of the early 1900s was one—when Ramonne had been tempted. But after World War II, Phuket seemed destined to be strip-mined and laid to waste as the tin barons plundered the island.

The heyday of sexual fantasy tourism in the latter part of

the past century was again somewhat intriguing to the vampire. It meant a plethora of easy victims. But on the one occasion that he did, in fact, escape the "heat"—the police—in Bangkok and head out of town, he went to Pattaya. Phuket had always seemed too far and hardly worth the effort. But he had recently resurrected his old profession, and hitmen go where they are assigned. When Ping Narong told Ramonne that he needed him to take care of a job in Phuket, he willingly obliged.

After all, he owed Ping Narong. This debt could never be repaid. No price could be placed on it.

He literally owed his life—his existence—to Ping Narong.

Ramonne's past reincarnations had been arduous and miraculous. He had voluntarily allowed his only friend in the world —Martin Larue—to blow his head off with a shotgun on hallowed ground—the Temple of the Dawn. What was left was incinerated by the rising sun and turned to ash.

But Charoen, a blind fortune-teller, had been in pursuit of the vampire and had collected what remained of the vampire's ashes and painfully regenerated Ramonne in a bat-infested cave.

In modern-day Angkor, he defeated his ancient enemy, the Chinese vampire who had originally laid the blood curse on him, and had persecuted the Cambodian lands ever since. That battle and the subsequent metamorphosis found him actually allowed brief forays into the sunlight for the first time in a century and a half.

But this didn't last, and led to the demise of his creation— the female vampire Kanchana.

Upon his return to Bangkok, his friend Martin was in trouble. Japanese "Black Dragon" agents—World War II spies now aligned with the Yakuza—mistakenly believed that Ramonne was in possession of an ancient powerful relic that gave him eternal life. The Oracle.

They kidnapped Martin's pregnant wife and—conjuring up

a fiery dragon—were ready to sacrifice her and their unborn child on a sacred altar.

It took all of Ramonne's strength and power to defeat the demon force Rakshasa that was drawn forth to carry out this dastardly deed. Ramonne vanished in the fallout from the fierce battle.

———

But Ramonne endured.

He had been trapped in a netherworld—neither a spirit nor a soul. Not mortal or immortal—just ethereal.

He'd been aware of his surroundings—in the sense that it was dark or light, cool or warm, wet or dry.

Time meant nothing. His ethereal self floated through time—hours, days, months, years, eons—none of it mattered.

Without any sense of time, it was hard to know when it happened.

But *this much* Ramonne knew.

It was dark, it was humid, and suddenly the silence was replaced by noise.

Explosions! *One, two…three.* Like volcanoes erupting. And then, time and space returned in a *flash.*

Ramonne Delacroix *existed* again. So did the world around him. He was lying on a filthy pavement. In a puddle…A puddle of blood.

As his eyes slowly focused, he saw three pairs of shoes encircling him. As his ears became attuned, he heard voices… speaking in Thai.

"*Rain a rak*? What the fuck?"

A second voice: "Who the fuck is this?"

Ramonne became aware that he was naked, lying in a fetal position—in a pool of blood. He slowly turned his head to face the source of the voices.

"Shit." Three men stared down at Ramonne. Each wore a long trench coat and carried a pistol pointed at him.

One turned his head and spoke into the darkness. "*Hua na…* you should see this."

An older man stepped out of the shadows. He looked down at Ramonne. A look of astonishment. "Jao Nai?"

Ramonne recognized the man. "Khun Ping. Jao Phor." He put his hands together in a *wai*—the Thai symbol of respect.

The man, Ping Narong, turned to the man next to him. "Sun. Cover him."

Sun took off his long coat and draped it over Ramonne's shoulders. Ramonne pushed his arms through the sleeves and wrapped it around him.

"Help him up."

Two of the men extended their arms, and Ramonne slowly stood up.

"Where am I?"

"Lat Phrao," Ping replied. "Please, step out of that bloody mess."

Ramonne looked down. He'd forgotten about the puddle of blood.

"Is that mine?"

"No. We just dispatched Somchai Suwanaphan. May he rot in hell."

"But…where's the body?"

Ramonne stared at the puddle. It slowly began curdling, and within a few minutes it was gone.

Ping Narong and his men instinctively reached for the heavy gold amulets that hung around each of their necks, as they waved their pistols.

Ramonne was lost in thought.

"Jao Nai?" Ping nervously spoke. "What happened here?"

It was several moments before Ramonne turned and spoke. "I have a theory." He wrapped the coat around him against the night's sudden chill. "Let's get out of here and I'll tell you. I'm extremely thirsty."

———

Martin left the penthouse shortly after nine that evening. In the cool marble lobby he was warmly greeted by Nong the security guard, and Virit the doorman. He stopped and chatted in Thai with Virit before walking up the short sub-*soi* to Soi Langsuan. Martin had lived on the fashionable street for nearly thirty years. It was centrally located. It was walking distance to the American Embassy and several major shopping malls. There were jazz clubs and excellent restaurants. Gaggan, a Michelin-starred Indian restaurant was across the street until just recently.

It was Friday evening, and Martin was headed—as he often did—to the Foreign Correspondents' Club, the FCC. This institution was H.Q. to the various expat reporters, journalists, and writers who called Southeast Asia in general, and Bangkok in particular, home. On Friday evenings a mellow sort of jazz was played, and Martin had a regular table reserved for him and several friends.

Martin stayed on the east side of the street instead of crossing over as he normally would because of massive construction taking place 24 hours a day, and which had a quarter of the block under constant attack. The forty-story structure was being assembled one floor at a time—with giant cranes lifting the completed sections into place.

Martin loathed the path the city was hell-bent upon—out with the old, in with the new. When he had moved into his penthouse apartment, the sixteen-story building was considered a skyscraper. Now it was dwarfed by the gleaming towers and constant construction that interrupted his views. He knew that eventually they would be moving. He wasn't sure where to, but he knew his days on charming Langsuan were numbered.

The noise from the construction was deafening and Martin put his Audio Technica noise cancelling ear buds in, and cranked up his Spotify playlist. To keep the dust to a minimum, all open sites were required to be screened in, and the finished floors were sheathed in green netting. Strings of wire and dangling bare bulbs lit the framework as dozens of Burmese and Cambodian workers in open-toed sandals and yellow hard hats climbed the girders and beams.

Martin made it to Ploenchit Road and turned left. The old Maneeya Center building was just a block away, and soon he was ascending to the club.

It was already Christmas at the FCC. Kittisak, the bartender, in his stiff tuxedo uniform, sported a Santa hat, as did the waitresses. As usual, Bob was at the piano. "Night in Tunisia" was being interpreted, and the chatter was kept low in respect. Bob was known to throw a plate or an ashtray at those who ignored him.

Martin joined a small, slightly inebriated group of expats, and ordered a Heineken. Colin McGavin, a hard-drinking novelist and freelance journalist, was the first to greet him.

"Martin Larue. Come to see what the hoi polloi are up to?"

"Just in the mood for some Christmas cheer." He nodded to the others at the table. "Gentlemen…what's new in the kingdom?"

"Sobriety. The latest sin tax has just come into effect. Kittisak's pissed off. He just printed new menus and now he has to change all the drink prices again. And you can actually be arrested for taking a selfie with a beer and posting it online," said John Grady.

"You mean like this?" Lincoln Thomas snapped a pic of himself chugging a pint of Guinness.

"Nobody will give a shit if you post that on your Facebook page—but if you're a little Thai soap opera star, you could be jailed and fined, like those half-dozen celebrities last week."

"Yeah, that's the temperance movement. The government is

courting them. But do you seriously believe they'd outlaw liquor *and* prostitution. Tell me, who's going to come here, then?" Colin interjected.

Martin shrugged and sipped his beer. "I think it's all just grandstanding. Making a big show of their concern over the moral turpitude that invades the dark side of the kingdom. I don't believe they're serious about any of this."

And with that the evening's tone was set.

————

"You know who I am."

Ping Narong stated: "Yes...*phi tai hong*. Ghost who drinks blood."

Ramonne smiled. "Close enough."

They were in Ping's office on Sukhumvit Soi 33—once known as the "street of dead artists" due to the proliferation of hostess bars with names such as Gauguin, Matisse, and Picasso. Now it seemed just another faceless *soi*—condos, apartments, massage parlors. In reality, Ping Narong owned the entire street. *Jao phor* meant "Godfather," and that's who he was. Ping Narong's hand was everywhere. Gambling, prostitution, drugs, arms trading, oil smuggling, stolen gems, poaching, logging, endangered species. If it was illegal, he was involved. He rigged elections. He secured lucrative contracts for big businesses, and he bribed government officials to obtain prime land deals. He even ran legitimate, though admittedly shady, businesses: nightclubs, go-go bars, and snooker halls.

He was the man to contact when you needed something fixed. Or broken. Ramonne had been invaluable to him. Before his banishment from the astral plane, Ramonne had been Ping's favorite hitman—due to his enviable invincibility. The vampire performed the tasks out of boredom.

Ramonne was now dressed in a loose-fitting suit provided by one of Ping's henchmen. Mekhong whiskey was being passed around while Ramonne sipped from a claret Ping had kept especially for the vampire.

"The English word is *vampire*. The living dead." He sipped his wine. "There are ways to destroy a vampire, but when this happens, their essence or soul, or whatever you'd call it, doesn't actually move on anywhere. It keeps hanging out in the world, which means they never truly die. It also means that, if someone has the knowledge and the resources to do so, they are able to reunite the body of the vampire in question with the spirit, through necromantic rituals."

Ping and his men were puzzled.

"Necromantic rituals?" Ping queried.

"Casting spells. Calling on black forces through chanting and sacrifices.

"Ahhh. *Sek khatha*." Ping nodded.

"My spirit, my *ka*, was placed in the body of Somchai Suwanaphan. That was not an accident. This means there is a necromancer here in Bangkok who has resurrected me…for a purpose, no doubt."

"Jao Nai, it wasn't me. But I am glad to have you back." He poured a strong shot of Mekhong and added soda to his glass. "And I do have a job for you, if you are interested."

Ramonne raised his glass and they toasted.

Kamala. Ramonne liked the name.

He liked Kamala. The little village wasn't Patong—the stinking sludge pit by the sea that his van had mysteriously passed through earlier in the evening. His driver was under the mistaken impression that Ramonne would appreciate its abundance of neon and wall-to-wall crap. Ramonne glanced through the heavily-tinted windows at the destination center—Soi Bangla—and then spoke the first words of the journey.

"Our business—is it here?"

"No, Jao Nai," the driver respectfully replied. "I thought you'd want to see the red-light district. Everyone does."

Ramonne scowled. "Do I *look* like a tourist?"

The black van sped along the crowded seashore and up over a series of hills. Soon, Ramonne was in another vehicle. This one was white and had no doors. It was like a golf cart on steroids, and it took the vampire up another steep hill, this one luxuriously landscaped. It stopped at a massive villa overlooking Phuket's famous "Millionaire Mile"—so named for the valuable sea-view property.

The villa was 2,000 square meters of teak and marble. Ramonne thought it was a bit pretentious for him to occupy alone, but then he decided that his nearly two centuries on this Earth gave him a sense of entitlement that mere mortals didn't possess. He relaxed, changed his clothes, and took in the view.

Within thirty minutes his contact arrived. He handed Ramonne a slim aluminum case, bowed, and left.

It was Ping Narong's modus operandi that none of his agents knew anything about their target until they were safely embedded.

Ramonne dialed the code and opened the case. A photo of a muscular, heavily-tanned man stared back at him. His head was shaved clean like a cue ball.

Russian. Dimitri Kirilov. Nickname "Eddie." International arms trader.

There were a half-dozen more pictures—at various nightclubs in Europe and Russia. Two pages gave Ramonne the details he needed.

In the bottom of the case were three gold bars. Ramonne shut the case and locked it. He took out a slim lighter and burned the photos and paperwork.

In Ramonne's head, Dimitri Kirilov was now the *target*.

Just another seedy tropical bar. Two pool tables, a half-dozen plump whores, and a half-dozen foreign "geezers." Ramonne liked this word.

He's unreachable. Except for when he visits a small bar where he insists that his bodyguards remain while he spends a half-hour in a locked room with a local whore. This is the only available window of opportunity.

Ramonne sat at the bar. He had ordered a glass of red wine, but he hadn't touched it. One sniff had been enough.

The music was becoming annoying. He had turned off his vampire radar—the cacophony was too much. Occasional classic rock—especially from that renaissance known as the sixties—was acceptable to Ramonne's ears, but the rest offended him to the point that he reached across the bar with a 1,000-baht note on which he had written one word: "Queen." The girl understood and slipped the bill into her ample bosom. Soon, Freddie Mercury's distinctive voice singing "Bohemian Rhapsody" filled the timber hut.

The target was shooting pool with his lady friend. He was quite drunk. The woman seemed to care little for him. Her arm was draped listlessly over his shoulder. He mainly cared about his drink. He put his pool cue down and walked to the bar.

"*Potaskushka.* I ask for Absolute vodka." He smelled the glass and snorted. "This is piss. Let me see the bottle."

The girl shrugged and handed it to him. He took one sniff and snorted again. "*Pizdobal.*" He threw the bottle against the wall. It exploded.

The bar went silent. Only Freddie Mercury said anything.

One obvious bodyguard at the bar put his hand on the bulge at the back of his untucked Hawaiian shirt. The other, leaning against the black BMW parked at the curb, crushed out his cigarette and reached in his jacket pocket.

A very large woman emerged from the kitchen.

"Eddie."

She walked, arms extended, and embraced the target. She hugged him to her and kissed his bald head.

The silence ended. Everyone relaxed. Hands slid away from weapons.

"Why you cause such a scene?"

The target looked at her with baleful eyes. "You weren't here. They tried to serve me rotgut."

"I'm here now." She snapped her fingers. A fresh bottle of Absolute appeared from beneath the bar, the seal unbroken. The *mamasan* poured a tumbler glass full of the clear liquid and handed it to the target. Pacified, for the moment, he and his whore returned to the pool table.

Ramonne's boss had a vendetta with this man. Otherwise the vampire wouldn't be here. Large sums of money—Dubai skyscraper large—had to be involved. In the *real* world —Moscow, London—a target such as this would be unreachable. But here, in the tropics, he felt invincible. He threw caution to the wind.

Ping Narong did his work anonymously through international channels so that his targets had no idea who he was or where he was. They did business with his connections in Paris, London, or New York—they had no idea he was based in Bangkok.

"*Hooy na ny.* No fucking way!" The target threw his pool cue onto the table as the girl sunk the eight ball. She smiled.

Ramonne smiled too. *You'll never beat a bargirl at a game she plays every night.*

The target latched his arm around the girl and motioned to his goon at the bar. The pair stumbled towards the kitchen. They turned right at a little corridor marked with a "Toilet" sign.

Ramonne got up from the bar. He walked to the deck over-looking the street. The bodyguard was smoking, again.

Ramonne approached. He produced a cigarette. "Light?"

Automatically, a lighter was extended. Ramonne crushed the man's larynx before a sound could emerge. He opened the trunk of the BMW and within seconds there was no trace of the first bodyguard.

He returned to the bar. He made a decision about the second bodyguard, and walked determinedly to the toilet hallway. As he expected, the man got off his bar stool and followed.

Ramonne waited just outside the room, which had a picture of Elvis indicating it was the men's room; across the way, Marilyn Monroe identified the ladies' room.

The man came around the corner and Ramonne broke his neck.

He stuffed this one in the men's room and hung an "Out of order" sign on the locked door. He waited a moment, determined no one else was approaching, and moved down the hallway.

The sounds emerging from the other side of the corrugated plastic door were about what he expected. A bit exaggerated, but the act of primeval pleasure is often difficult to overhear.

He pushed the door. It yielded with very little resistance, coming completely off its hinges and falling into the room.

The room looked pretty much as he expected, too. A cheap bed with a soiled bedspread dominated the tight space. A fluorescent light cast a garish green glow over its occupants.

However, besides the whore and the target, there was an unexpected third person. A teenage girl was spread-eagled naked on the bed—her hands tied to two ringbolts in the faded plaster wall. The target, naked as well, was astride her.

The whore was holding the younger girl's legs. She was the first to turn to Ramonne. Hers was a look of annoyance.

"Get out," she spat.

Ramonne took a moment to force the tortured door back into the frame. Then the target turned his bald head. His look was more than annoyance. It was a look Ramonne was intimately familiar with.

Ravishment. Gluttony. Rapaciousness.

Blood dripped from the corners of his mouth and ran from open wounds on the girl's neck. His eyes glowed with a yellow cast.

'What do you want?'

The words were not spoken. But Ramonne heard them all the same. He replied in kind.

'I'm here to kill you.'

The target moved rapidly. He was off the girl and standing in front of Ramonne in an instant. He glowered at Ramonne. This time his lips moved as he spoke.

"Kill me?" He laughed. "Do you know how many have tried that?"

Ramonne replied, "No."

"Dozens. Do you know where they are now?"

Ramonne didn't bother to reply.

"In their graves."

While this brief exchange was taking place, the whore had moved behind Ramonne. She had a fire axe hidden under the bed, and she moved to strike. Without looking back at her, Ramonne seized the hand and then turned and buried the axe in her forehead.

She slumped to the floor.

"Impressive." The target smiled, his hands now on his hips. Ramonne tossed him his trousers.

The target pulled them on and then extracted a cigarette pack from a pocket. He offered the pack to Ramonne, who declined.

He lit the cigarette and sat on the bed. He had to move the girl's right leg. The girl groaned slightly. He ignored her and motioned to a plastic chair under the air-conditioner. Ramonne sat down.

"So...you're a pro. You're fast, I'll give you that."

"You don't understand, do you?"

"You've been sent by Ping Narong. He's annoyed over the stolen arms shipment to Afghanistan. He suspects me."

Ramonne shrugged. "That's not my business."

"Let me finish this cigarette and we'll step outside and settle this like men."

"We're not *men*. And we'll settle it here."

The target seemed to have an epiphany. He crushed out his cigarette.

"Who are you?"

"A forsaken one. An immortal."

The target's yellow eyes glowed. "You can't be."

"Why not? You are."

"Then you must know you can't kill me."

Ramonne smiled. His eyes had the same amber glow.

"Oh…but I can."

Ramonne had fought another vampire before. Just once. In Angkor. That beast had been over a thousand years old and his strength was enormous. The battle had nearly cost Ramonne his existence.

This one was young. He was sure of it. Probably no more than a half-century of immortality. But still he must possess the strength of a dozen mortals. Best to be cautious. Let him strike first.

He didn't have to wait long. The target sprang at Ramonne, now with the axe in hand. He moved so fast that no one could have seen him remove the blade from the dead whore.

But Ramonne saw it. And reacted. He ducked a potentially decapitating blow, and dove into the man's midsection. The force was akin to a bulldozer ramming a wall. He pushed the target through the tarpaper-covered window and into a muddy canal outside. They plunged together into the murky water.

To kill an immortal, there must first be a decapitation. This renders the beast immobile—but not for long.

Does the target know this? Ramonne suspected he did. Perhaps he belongs to a Russian covenant. A clan. They would have shared such knowledge.

Ramonne was a loner. He had met exactly one other immortal in his life, other than two short-lived changelings that he created—with disastrous results. His own creator —Zhoupeng—taught him only that he must feed on fresh blood and he must avoid sunlight. The rest Ramonne had learned in his eternal existence. His world was devoid of other immortals —or so he thought.

They struggled in the water for at least ten minutes. Holding their breath made no difference. They didn't need oxygen. They received their sustenance through blood alone. But they would not function at full capacity without eventually taking oxygen directly into their lungs—so they both broke the surface. They each lay immobile for a few moments, slowly drifting to the beach, where the brackish water would merge with the sea.

'Why?''The target spoke through his thoughts.

'Why what?' Ramonne replied.

'Why do you wish to destroy me?'

'It's not personal.'

'Bullshit.'

'It's a job.'

'So…you do work for Ping Narong.'

'Does it matter?'

'Yes. It fucking matters.'

The target straightened himself in the muddy canal. Ramonne did the same. They faced each other, treading water.

The target motioned with his arm as he spoke. "I come to this place for pleasure. It is one of a few ports of call where I can receive sustenance without fear of reprisals."

Ramonne understood. For a century and a half Ramonne had relied on the Bangkok police to clean up after him—for a fee. He assumed the target had a similar arrangement here.

"And you would deny me that?"

"That has nothing to do with why I'm here."

They were slowly drifting closer and closer to the sea. A motor from a returning fishing boat was getting louder. The water grew shallow and finally both men stood in the mud.

Ramonne was tired of talking. He started walking. The target followed. The thick sludge and silt made it slow going.

"If you'd stand still for a moment, we could figure this out." The target yelled over the boat's increasing volume.

'Nothing to figure out. I told you, this isn't personal.'

The target was gaining on Ramonne, who had his back to him as he walked slowly to the spot where the canal joined the sea, where the longtail fishing boat was slowly returning to the shore.

Longtail boats were the standard fishing vessels in the area. The motor was mounted in a manner that allowed the pilot to maneuver in shallow water by leaning on a handle that pivoted the long shaft of the propeller to whatever depth he desired.

The fisherman was oblivious to the two figures who were now in the surf as he coaxed his craft to shore.

'Do you enjoy yourself?' Ramonne stopped and addressed the target.

'Enjoy myself?'

'Yes. Do you enjoy yourself?'

'Of course I enjoy myself. I fuck, I drink, I kill…I don't die.'

'That's it?'

'What else is there?'

Ramonne smiled. "You're lucky I'm here."

"I'm lucky? Stand still, you cunt, and I'll show you who's lucky."

The fisherman had just thrown his anchor over the bow, and the target had caught it. He now brandished the heavy metal claw, swinging it by its chain.

Ramonne turned his back on the target as he made his way to the stern. "I offer you something that was once offered to me. I took it willingly."

"And what is that?" As the target said the words, he flung the anchor at Ramonne.

Ramonne merely ducked. As he did, he grabbed the shaft of the motor and swung it with tremendous force. The rotating blade cut through the cartilage and bone and completely severed the target's head.

"Freedom," Ramonne spoke. "I offer you freedom."

The sun rose right on cue. The monks had preceded it by thirty minutes. Their chanting in the seaside temple began, as always, at six a.m. Every morning the low, musical drone crept into the hills of Millionaire Mile. However, very few of its slumbering residents ever heard it.

Ramonne, in particular, never heard it. He had checked out of the villa in the middle of the night and was safely ensconced in the back of his luxury van on the return trip to Bangkok, well before the first monk set his bare foot onto the temple floor.

By 6:15 there were two dozen shaven-headed, orange-robed monks on their knees chanting their magical, musical rhythms. But midway into the ceremony, Khun Pho noted a disturbing commotion from the temple dogs. Usually they slept through the prayers. But they were definitely aroused. The noise was deafening. He bowed and then rose to his feet and descended the temple stairs.

Outside, the dogs were in a frenzy—fighting over what appeared to be freshly barbecued meat.

Where did it come from?

Khun Pho puzzled over this until a chunk of grizzle hit him on the shoulder.

He looked up.

Something was frying on the temple roof.

As Ramonne slept, he dreamed of dragging the corpse and the head on to the deserted beach. He smiled with irony when he spotted the golden spires of the temple across the beach road. "Hallowed ground." The morning sun would incinerate the body and the target would exist no more.

Ramonne awoke with a start. Not something he normally did.

He had had a bad dream. He dreamed of a Russian covenant of vampires running amok in Phuket. What was it that made him think the Russian was not alone?

As he had assessed, the target was obviously a very young vampire. His strength was scarcely equal to that of Ramonne. But he had known of the vampire's way. This meant he had been educated by another immortal.

Ramonne was well aware of the recent Russian influx into Phuket. Was this the first wave of Russian vampires?

Ramonne spent the rest of the night in fitful sleep, punctuated by disturbing dreams.

3

"It's literally a cesspool now. After they demolished all the restaurants and the beach clubs, the local government built septic tanks twenty feet from the shoreline. A three hundred million baht project that never worked. *Ten million* US dollars. They overflow every couple months and turn the water black."

"I'm not surprised—all the beaches are polluted. But, seriously, they tore down the Catch Club?"

Martin was still in discussion with Colin McGavin, who had just returned from a quick trip to Phuket. They had been talking for a couple hours and consumed a half-dozen beers each.

"Yeah. Apparently everyone thought they'd clear the southern end of the squatters and illegal structures on the beach —but certainly not Catch.

Colin finished his beer and signaled for another round.

"But they bulldozed it, just like everything else."

"Amazing…What about all the 'World's Best Beach Club' awards?"

"Apparently the word came down from Bangkok. Clear the beach. Back to nature. The tourists be damned."

Martin shook his head. "Surin was my favorite beach. It was

crowded, sure, but it was Catch, and the two or three really good restaurants that made it special."

"Well it ain't special anymore. Like I said, it's literally a cesspool. Nothing but low-rent tourists with bags from 7-Eleven, and Thai family picnics. There's no garbage disposal in place, and the trash just builds up and eventually blows into the sea."

"So much for back to nature."

"What do you care? You're rich. You'll go to the Amanpuri."

"Actually, we prefer Trisara. So close to the airport and yet completely isolated."

"Yeah, you and Mick Jagger. Actually, Trisara has its own problems—seems half of the villas are on national forest land."

The state of political affairs in the kingdom was the source of most of the conversation at the FCC. In Martin's thirty-year residency he'd seen three military coups and he'd stopped counting the number of regime changes. Currently the country was in its fifth year of military rule. It was supposed to be a constitutional monarchy with a king and an elected government. But rival factions became so heatedly divided that Bangkok was regularly under siege with tens of thousands of protestors camping at major intersections and disrupting traffic and people's lives for years. Finally, in 2014 the military took over—once again—and declared martial law, suspending elections, and running the country like a benevolent dictatorship.

Martin found that this had little effect on his personal life, but he was not a fan of the suspension of personal freedoms and the muzzling of the press. It was not uncommon at the FCC's weekly guest speaker evenings to have visitors from the military, and often these events were cancelled before they took place due to political pressure.

Conversation at the FCC was often about politics—Thai or foreign. The banter over Phuket's demise as a tropical paradise was considered political because it seemed mired in corruption.

"What were you doing in Phuket?" Martin asked Colin.

"Chasing a story for the *Times*."

Martin's late father was a newspaper magnate who, when he passed away, left much of his fortune to Martin. One of the remaining papers was the *Bangkok Times*.

"Who sent you—Prakasan?"

"Yes."

"How is the old goat?"

"Good. I think he misses you."

Martin doubted that. Prakasan had been a city-desk editor those many years ago, who had suggested that Martin go on the ill-fated police ride-along that led to a visit by the vampire, and, after a terrifying ordeal, the beginning of a very bizarre friendship.

"What's the story?"

"Right up your alley. As I recall, you have a morbid interest in the bizarre."

"Not exactly…What is it?"

"A temple in Kamala. Seems the dogs went crazy during the dawn prayers, and, when the monks investigated, there was a human body adorning the apex of the temple roof. The monk who climbed the ladder said it was a foreigner. But here's the creepy part. As soon as he reached a stick to drop it to the ground—it burst into flame. Soon there was nothing left but some blackened rib bones. Kind of like my plate when I leave Tony Roma's."

McGavin laughed but Martin was frozen.

"When was this?"

"About two weeks ago—"

"No. What time of day?"

"Dawn."

This terrified Martin. He was immediately transported back to a morning seventeen years ago at the Temple of Dawn when he witnessed Ramonne's corpse burst into flame as the first rays of the sun lit upon it. Thus the vampire ceased to exist. That is, until he was resurrected by the blind fortune-teller.

"The police were involved?"

"Yeah, kind of. They declared it a suicide of an unidentified male *farang*."

"Suicide?"

"Martin, you've been here long enough. You know that all unexplained *farang* deaths are declared suicides. The dozens of men who fall or are pushed off hotel balconies, the shootings and stabbings that have no apparent motive, the hangings…all suicides."

"What did you conclude?"

"Apparently there was a commotion in a rough-and-tumble bar by a canal that runs alongside the temple. Several witnesses saw a Russian and a Frenchman get into a fight. They pitched over the rail and into the filthy water and were apparently swept out to sea. The Russians I interviewed denied any knowledge of this, and no one—Russian or French—was reported missing."

The color drained from Martin's face at the mention of a Frenchman. Could it be that—once again—Ramonne had been resurrected? It had now been nine years since he had sacrificed himself in a metaphysical battle with a spirit that was summoned by an ancient talisman sought by a Japanese Black Dragon agent who thought he was seeking his own immortality. Could it be possible that the vampire had again been reborn only to perish on Phuket?

"So…what does your story say? What happened?"

"Damned if I know. I didn't write a story. Prakasan simply ran the two-paragraph wire service release that said an unidentified corpse was found incinerated at a temple on Phuket. Subsequently ruled a suicide by the local authorities…*Amazing Thailand* indeed."

———

It was going on midnight when Martin returned to the sanctuary of his penthouse. He was surprised to find an enormous silver evergreen wreath mounted on the front door.

When he stepped inside he was greeted by festive candleholders and lanterns in the entryway. There were a dozen matching sets in elegant shades of gold and deep red. The candles that flickered in the holders were all electrical with wavering "flames."

The dining room table now sported a formal Christmas centerpiece with romantic red roses surrounded by white tallow berries displayed in silver vases made to resemble birch bark. They reflected the warm light from more electric candles and the rich reds from the flowers. Pieces of boxwood garland and sprigs of berries surrounded the bases of the vases.

Areeya had been busy.

———

"His girlfriend is coming for the holidays."

Martin put down his paper and looked at his wife.

"His *girlfriend*? I didn't realize he had a girlfriend."

"Neither did I."

Breakfast was generally a casual affair in the Larue household. If it was a school day, Nina and Areeya ate together, and then On, Martin's driver, took her to school. Martin had no particular schedule, and usually fended for himself while his wife took care of the running of the house.

Martin had arrived home fairly late following his Friday night ritual, and had risen accordingly. Areeya came into the parlor as he was on his second cup of Earl Grey. After delivering her news, she sat opposite him.

"Who is she?"

"Juliette. She's French."

"Where did they meet?"

"Paris, of course."

"Of course…Anything more?"

"Not much. They're in love."

"Of course." Martin sipped his tea and thought about this. "When does she arrive?"

"Tomorrow."

"*Tomorrow?*"

"Yes."

"And he just told you?"

Martin put his cup down. "A little more notice would have been nice."

"I agree. But your son—"

"*Our* son."

"Our son is not used to doing things in a normal manner. In that regard, he takes after his father."

"*Touché.*"

"Anyway, she will be at the airport at seven tomorrow evening. Hon would like us to pick her up."

"Of course. He'll be with us…yes?"

"No. Rehearsals."

Martin pushed his chair back and crossed his arms. "Let me get this straight. His girlfriend, who we've never heard of before, is arriving from Paris to spend the Christmas holidays with us, and we are expected to pick her up without him because he is in rehearsals for his first recording sessions?"

Areeya nodded. "Yes. That's about right."

Martin shook his head. "When did we lose control?"

Areeya smiled. "A long time ago."

———

It was several hours later when Hon finally arose.

He appeared in the kitchen and grabbed a coffee pot and poured a cup.

"Good morning, sunshine." Martin was seated at the kitchen table, going through his mail.

"Hey, what's up?" Hon remarked.

"You, for one thing." Martin looked at his watch. "Two o'clock…Who are you? Elvis?"

Hon smiled. "You're showing your age, Dad."

"What is it with musicians and late nights?"

"I don't know. Music just isn't a *morning* thing. You know?"

"No, I don't. But I expect it has to do with freedom of expression, inhibition…things like that."

"There you go." Hon sat down next to Martin.

"Are you hungry? I could fry some eggs."

Hon laughed. "You, *cook*? Really? You've never cooked anything for me."

"Well, I was actually going to get Soon to do it." Soon was their Burmese maid. "But…yes, I *do* cook. Especially breakfast. I was a bachelor for many years, and cooking breakfast is an art that a bachelor needs to learn. My scrambled eggs are spectacular."

Hon smiled. "I'm sure they are, but I've got to get to the studio. I have two solos to get down before the trio comes in this evening. There'll be food there."

Hon started to stand, and Martin put a hand on his arm. "Before you go…Tell me about Juliette."

"Ah…yes. Juliette." He smiled. "You'll like her. I know you will. She's French."

"Yes. I heard."

"She's not just French. She's *really* French. All the quirks."

He leaned against the kitchen counter and crossed his arms. "She's a gourmet. A wine snob. Dresses with flair in a Bohemian way. Doesn't suffer bores. Speaks English but with a very annoying French accent. And we are very much in love."

Hon slung his Hugo Boss leather bag over his shoulder and picked an apple out of a silver bowl. "I really have to go."

Martin watched him leave with a sigh. *Oh to be eighteen and in love.*

He returned to his papers, but he found that he couldn't concentrate. In the back of his mind he heard Colin McGavin describing a corpse that burst into flames with the dawn's light.

4

———

December

"Martin Larue, as I live and breathe. Is it really you?"

The office hadn't changed. The large desk was overflowing with papers, and several tables held the next day's newspaper's galleys, laid out sequentially.

"Prakasan. You old dog. How are you?" Martin templed his hands and bowed at the waist, only to be hugged and kissed on each cheek—an unusual greeting from an Indian, but Prakasan was an unusual man. Martin recalled that Prakasan had always seemed ageless to him, with his bald pate that a dozen jet-black strands of hair were drawn across. They were still there, though they were a shade of gray now. But the twinkling smile and the dimples were unchanged.

Martin pointed to the office door, which stood open. "I see that you are *managing* editor now. Congratulations."

"What are 'words'? Without a salary increase, it means very little."

"I can look into it, if you'd like," Martin offered.

"Nonsense. You and I go to back to when your father brought you here holding your little hand. I was a copy boy then. I'm satisfied with my lot in life…But what brings you here?"

"A story. Something Colin McGavin told me."

"Ah, Colin. What did that rogue tell you?"

"He said you sent him to Phuket to follow up on a mysterious *farang* death."

"The temple in Kamala. What did Colin say?"

"He said that the reason you sent him was because of the rumor. That the body was found on the temple roof, and when the monks tried to move it—at dawn—it burst into flames."

Prakasan sighed and sat down. He motioned for Martin to have a seat across from his desk.

"What you just said is preposterous. That's why I sent Colin there. To get to the truth."

"And what was the truth?"

"Without a police investigation there is no way to prove this, but…it seems a Frenchman and a Russian had a fight, and the Russian died. Apparently the Frenchman set the body on fire in an attempt to hide the crime."

"He hauled the body to the roof of a temple and set it on fire?"

Prakasan shrugged his shoulders. "I do not believe the body was ever on the temple roof. That makes no sense."

"None of this makes any sense."

"Martin. Every day I get stories that make no sense. You should know this. It wasn't that long ago when you were convinced you had uncovered a serial killer who had been operating unnoticed in Bangkok for over a dozen years. That made no sense."

Martin winced. He had never told Prakasan the truth, for he knew he would never believe it.

"You sent Colin to Phuket. You must have had some belief in what you were told."

"I sent Colin because I believed the person who called me about it."

"Who was that?"

"Jason. He's general manager of the *Phuket News*."

"You trust him."

"I do. He was told the story by one of his Thai reporters, who went to the temple and talked with the monks."

"Did he run the story?"

"No."

"Why not?"

"As he said to me, there was no story there. No photos of the burning corpse. And eventually no sign at all of a corpse. It completely turned to ash and blew into the wind."

"Do you have a file on it?"

"Yes. A slim one."

"May I borrow it?"

Prakasan got up and went to a bank of cabinets. He meticulously moved his right index finger down the labels until he found the drawer he wanted.

He handed the file to Martin. "As I said, there isn't much in here."

"Thank you, old friend."

Prakasan's head bobbled as he smiled. "Don't be such a stranger, Martin Larue."

———

Suvarnabhumi is one of two international airports serving Bangkok. It's pronounced "Soo-wan-a-poom" and means "Land of Gold." The name appears in many ancient Indian and Buddhist texts. The Thais traditionally refer to the boggy site thirty kilometers east of Bangkok as Nong Ngu Hao or "Cobra Swamp." Opened in 2006, it is already overburdened by the massive surge in air traffic though the region.

Martin, Areeya, and their driver On were waiting outside the international arrivals area with what seemed like a thousand others. On carried a clipboard on which Martin had written "Juliette." About thirty minutes after the announced arrival, the gates opened and the passengers from Air France began to appear. They pushed carts overflowing with bags, or they dragged bulging carry-on bags behind them.

Families, old couples, young couples, businessmen in Burberry coats, college boys and girls toting huge backpacks. They all seemed tired, haggard, and over-dressed from their twelve-hour flight from a cold land far to the west.

All except one. A very fashionable, very beautiful young woman. She walked with the confidence of a model. Her hair was chestnut brown and cut diagonally from the nape of her neck to a few inches below her chin. She wore a loose gray turtleneck cashmere tucked into a mid-length denim skirt with buttons up the front. A light wool topcoat was draped over her shoulders. Besides her leather handbag, she had one piece of luggage. It was a size larger than carry-on, and was brown and covered in the multiple patterns that distinguished it as Louis Vuitton and *tres* expensive. She didn't drag it behind her, but rolled it alongside her effortlessly with its wide upright handle.

"That's her," Martin exclaimed.

Areeya frowned. "How do you know?"

Martin smiled. "I know my son." He motioned for On to get to the front of the gate and make sure she would see the sign.

In the press of the crowd and the general chaos, they lost sight of On and her for a few moments. But soon he returned, the young lady following him. On was now rolling the Louis Vuitton.

"Juliette. How nice to finally meet you." Martin and Juliette exchanged kisses on the cheek, right to left. "This is my wife, Areeya."

"*Enchanté.*" Areeya had her hand out but Juliette surprised her with cheek kisses. "Thank you."

"How was the flight?" Martin asked.

"Long, *rasant*. Boring." With her thumb extended she waved

her right hand up and down alongside her face as if she were shaving.

Martin laughed. He'd forgotten how much the French used hand gestures to communicate their feelings. Areeya looked confused.

"Shall we go to the car?"

"*Mais oui*. I can't wait to see Hon."

"Hon, I'm afraid, is rehearsing."

"So? We go to the rehearsal. *Oui*?"

Martin thought about this a moment. "Okay...*oui*. We'll go."

———

Martin's black BMW Gran Tourer SUV pulled up to the Moonstar Studios guard gate at about 8:30. It is said in Thailand that if you drive a black Mercedes you will never be stopped by the police. Martin understood the philosophy—all politicians traveled in a black Mercedes, and the royal family had their own cream-colored version—but Martin preferred the BMW, and besides, he was rarely behind the wheel.

Although their name was not on any guest list, it was Areeya's maiden surname that got the gate raised.

Moonstar is a full service entertainment facility consisting of eight fully equipped sound stages of various sizes. Motion pictures such as *Bangkok Dangerous, Shanghai,* and *Hangover Part II* have utilized its massive stages, while music videos and Thai soap operas favor the smaller ones. Recently, concerts began to be held at Studio 8, with Death Cab for Cutie, Nine Inch Nails, and many others.

On was directed to Stage 4. He parked the car and Martin, Areeya, and Juliette were escorted into the canteen by Simon, a British lawyer who represented Blue Note, Hon's record label.

"Can I get you anything? A cup of tea? A glass of wine?"

"Hot tea would be nice." Martin smiled. "Earl Grey?"

"What else! And for the ladies?"

Areeya accepted a glass of wine, while Juliette dismissed Simon with a wave. "I have come a long way to see him."

Simon smiled. "Yes, of course. They should be taking a break soon—"

Juliette opened the stage door without waiting for further explanation.

Immediately a loud bell rang.

Inside, the relatively small studio space—twenty by thirty meters—had been made even smaller by a set-up of sound-proofing baffles. Three musicians—guitar, bass, and drums—flanked an ebony Yamaha grand piano. Hon was bent over the keys, totally entranced until the bell sounded.

He looked up. Annoyed. But then he saw Juliette.

"Juliette!" He stopped playing and went to her.

As the bell shut off, the other musicians also stopped playing and watched.

"My darling. How I've missed you." Juliette and Hon kissed for what seemed like an eternity to Martin and Areeya, who stood in the open doorway.

The guitar player put down his instrument and stretched. The bass player laid his big bass down carefully and lit a cigarette. The drummer stuck his sticks in a slot on the snare drum and lay down on the couch.

Hon and Juliette continued their embrace until they finally came up for air.

"Darling. Let me introduce you."

He took her by the hand and started with the guitar player. "This is John. He's American. Played with Jamie Cullum and Van Morrison. Also studied at the Royal Academy." John had long hair and a killer smile. He kissed Juliette's hand. She actually blushed a little.

"Ben plays the contra or upright bass. Protégé of Yo-Yo Ma. We met at the Berlin concert."

Ben was a slightly rotund black man in a stylish dark-green suit. He took her hand and squeezed it gently.

"And this is Nippy, our percussionist. Again, we met on the road. In Kyoto. He speaks six languages and plays over one hundred instruments—literally." Nippy, young and athletic with his hair tied back in a ponytail, bowed to Juliette.

The trio, giving knowing looks and smiling, started to pack up their instruments.

"Lads...what are you doing?" Simon raised his voice. "You've only just arrived."

John smiled and jerked a thumb toward the lovers. "So did she. Besides, we're all jet lagged. Let's get into it tomorrow."

Simon sighed and watched as Hon and Juliette walked out of the studio.

———

"He has his own driver now...? When did that start?" Areeya sat with Martin in the back of the BMW, an annoyed look on her face.

"I guess when rehearsals started. I don't know. I thought *you* paid attention to that sort of thing."

"He's *your* son."

"You keep saying that."

"Where do you think they're going?"

"I don't know. But don't worry...we've got the Louis Vuitton. She'll bring him back."

"I had Soon preparing a cassoulet in her honor."

"I'll be honored to try it."

"Too many calories for you. You get your regular sea bass."

Martin nodded. Once he'd turned forty, it seemed Areeya was determined to keep him fit, even if he wasn't. That meant white fish twice a week, no rice or pasta, lean meats, and no desserts.

Of course, that was what he was served at home. Since he was out of the house at least three evenings a week, she didn't have total control.

And then there was the wine.

Ramonne had taught him about wine. *When there is no wine…there is no love.*

He had a modest wine cellar with several word-class vintages.

At least he'd have a good Riesling with the sea bass.

————

The city of Bangkok gleamed in the night from the penthouse on the forty-second floor of the Emporium Suites. From here at night the cranes and half-finished structures were invisible—all you saw were the beautifully-lit towers.

Juliette's hands pressed against the floor to ceiling windows as Hon entered her. She let out a low moan and reached back to pull his face to her.

A bottle of champagne sat untouched in a silver bucket, and their clothing was strewn across the palatial suite.

The satin sheets of the oversized bed were a crumpled mess.

Hon shuddered and Juliette gasped and they both collapsed on the floor.

They stared into each other's eyes for a long moment and then finally Juliette spoke. *"Joyeux Noel, mon amour."*

Hon replied, "Merry Christmas to you also, my love." And they burst out laughing.

————

The file lay in Martin's lap. It had just three items.

There was a transcription of the phone call Prakasan received from Jason Beavan at the *Phuket News*. This was read and re-read by Martin. He was most interested in the account given by *Atikhan* Pho—a title earned in over thirty years of monastic service—to the reporter. The report stated that

...they were doing their morning prayers—chanting—when the incessant barking of the temple's stray dogs caused him to send some novices to stop them. When he got outside he saw the dogs fighting over what appeared to be pieces of raw meat. He tried to chase them away to stop the noise, when a chunk of offal landed at his feet.

He looked up and saw a dark shape on the temple eave. He got a tall bamboo ladder and climbed to investigate. At the very moment he arrived on the roof—the sun broke the horizon. He was horrified to see a rotting farang corpse. He prodded it with a tree branch and then it simultaneously burst into flame.

He cried out and the other monks stopped their chanting and hurried to the courtyard.

By now the flaming pieces had fallen to the ground and continued to burn until they melted to ash.

He heard Soon start the dishwasher, and Areeya getting Nina ready for bed, as he sat in the single glow of the reading light.

The other items in the file were Colin's expense account—he stayed at Andara, *the cheeky bastard*—and the police report, in Thai.

Martin read Thai, and it simply stated that a report was lodged of an incinerated corpse at the temple in Kamala, but when the officers arrived, there was no evidence of this, so there was no investigation.

As Martin closed the file, a single piece of paper fell out.

A sheet of Andara stationery with cursive handwriting. It said simply: "Something foul is afoot in Phuket."

Martin stuck the paper back in the file and closed it. He thought about calling Colin, but decided against it.

He poured himself another glass, sipped it, and sighed.

As had happened before, he was now torn with emotion. On one hand he welcomed the fact that if Ramonne had somehow been resurrected, he was now—apparently—re-exterminated.

His entry into Martin's life always meant chaos, death, and destruction.

On the other hand, the most extraordinary moments of his life had been in Ramonne's company. Ramonne's gift of thought transference—the ability to not only read another person's mind, but also to transfer his thoughts to you—had literally taken Martin hundreds of years back in time to the "discovery" of Angkor Wat and the coronations of ancient kings.

They had loved together, fought together, and more than once Ramonne had saved Martin's life and that of his family.

But it always had a price, and he was tired of the price.

He put the file down and was about to turn off the light when Areeya appeared. "She's taken our son."

"As I said…we have the Louis Vuitton. She won't get far."

He poured her a glass of wine.

"Where do you suppose they are?" she asked.

"In a good hotel. You really can't blame them."

"He knows we won't judge them. But I want them to stay here."

"And they will. They just need a little time together…alone. You remember what it was like, don't you?"

She sat on the arm of his big leather chair and put her head on his shoulder.

"I think so. Do you?"

Martin smiled and kissed her.

5

Professor Gerhardt Kaestle stretched and yawned. He had gone to bed at his usual hour, but he couldn't sleep. His afternoon nap was now a two-hour affair, taken in the late afternoon and lasting into the early evening. He attributed this to his now waking up in the middle of the night. Not unusual for a retired silver-haired man of eighty.

But the professor was a most unusual man. His field of practice was entomology—the study of insects. Mosquitos in particular. But the good professor had always held a belief in and fascination with other forms of "bloodsuckers"—in particular, vampires. His colleagues at Cornell University in Ithaca, New York laughed, but he persisted.

Over fifteen years ago, he was sought out by a young man with a horrific tale of an encounter with a vampire in Pattaya in Thailand, while on his honeymoon. The monster had stalked his bride and finally snatched and killed her. Driven mad with fury, the young man had battled the beast, who fled when a police helicopter descended on the scene. He realized later that the vampire had briefly bitten him. He had been mistakenly diagnosed with HIV, but the professor tested his blood and knew differently.

Mesmerized by the realization that he had finally found proof of the living dead's existence, he foolhardily injected himself with the tainted blood, and headed to Thailand in the hopes that either he would find the vampire or the vampire would find him.

In Bangkok, the latter occurred, and fortunately Ramonne listened to the professor's tale instead of merely dispatching him. This started the pair on a long and checkered path between Thailand and Cambodia, where Ramonne sought to destroy the thousand-year-old Chinese vampire who had "turned" him in 1860 and was the source of the virus that was then coursing through the professor's veins. *Destroy the source and you destroy the virus.*

It worked, and the professor was restored to vigorous good health.

Ramonne was not released from the curse that he had borne so long, but he did have a momentary reprise from his banishment to a life without the sun, and he briefly enjoyed the daylight hours.

For a time the professor managed the estate the vampire purchased in Siem Reap. Eventually, however, the vampire's escapades drew too much notice in such a rural environment, and they beat a hasty retreat back to Bangkok.

Here the vampire acquired an old two-story house on one of the quieter streets in one of the noisiest and most hectic cities in the world. The house on Sukhumvit Soi 8 had formerly been a French restaurant, and the large wine cellar suited both the vampire's slumbering habits and his palette.

Unfortunately, the battle to save Martin's wife and unborn daughter from sacrifice to the Japanese who were in possession of the Oracle that supposedly granted eternal life, ended with Ramonne dematerializing on the "sacred" pyre.

Martin and his family were safe, but the professor was left alone and grief-stricken.

He eventually sold the house on Soi 8 and moved

Ramonne's precious collection of art, antiques, and fine wines into storage.

He took up residence in a high-rise apartment on the Chao Phraya River.

His days were now filled with the joys of the elderly in good health—dining, long walks, and visits to new museums and galleries that had recently appeared.

That, and managing the vast fortune that the vampire had accumulated in almost two centuries of existence. The bulk of it was endowed to various charities—the only stipulation being that they not be associated with any religious organization or faith. The vampire's trust was known as the Ennomar Foundation, "Ennomar" being "Ramonne" spelled backwards.

He looked at his watch. Two a.m. *Why fight it?*

He got out of bed, poured himself a cognac, and opened his computer. He checked on the chat group he had joined several years ago, merely for amusement. It was a group of vampire fanatics who shared what they thought were "signs." Signs of the existence of that which they sought. But no matter how many leads were chased, it all came to naught. The professor remained anonymous and never revealed what he knew. He merely hoped that one day, again, there would be a sign. Something *real* for him to pursue.

But today, like most days, there was nothing new. Supposed sightings in Romania. *Why is it always Romania? Blame Bram Stoker, of course. And Egypt? Blame Anne Rice.*

He closed the file and went onto his balcony. The traffic on the river never came to a halt, and a long string of rice barges, bare bulbs strung from bow to stern, floated serenely southward. The professor tamped his pipe and topped up the tobacco. As he lit the match—

"Filthy habit."

In the match's glow, he saw…Ramonne.

He froze, not believing what he was seeing. The match finally burned his finger and he dropped it.

"My God…Is it really you?"

Ramonne smiled. "I suspect God has very little to do with it…but yes, *c'est moi*."

Tears of joy came to the professor's eyes.

"I can't believe it. I've prayed for this day."

"Again, I think you were calling on the wrong deity."

"Come inside."

———

After an hour or so, Ramonne had briefed the professor on what he knew about his resurrection and his strange encounter in Phuket.

"You seriously believe there are more of his kind in Phuket?"

"He was young, but he knew of the *ways*. He had been educated by another. Not merely abandoned as I was, to fend and learn for myself."

The professor poured them each a glass of Barolo. Ramonne smiled as he took the glass. "How is my wine cellar?"

"Your wines are safe, as are all your belongings. But of course, you know that don't you?"

Ramonne smiled. Of course he knew. Since his awakening, it had taken a while for him to totally regain his powers. Once he returned to the site of the old house on Soi 8, it had been easy for him to follow the trail of the professor over the past nine years. What had transpired was revealed to him, and there was no need for the professor to explain anything to the vampire.

"I keep a small amount of the wines for my own use. And I also continue the investments in wine futures, as you taught me, so the cellar is always replenished. In case…"

The vampire smiled. "In case of my return."

They clinked their glasses.

"Thank you, my friend. And thank you for taking care of my trust. You've done what I asked."

They swallowed and each leaned back in their chairs. Reflecting on this moment in silence.

Finally the professor spoke. "What of master Larue? Will you see him?"

"I don't know. He, perhaps, is better off without me."

"You know of his son? He's quite famous."

"Hon. That little boy?"

"He's eighteen."

Ramonne laughed. "Of course he is. No, I have not checked on Martin or his family. Tell me."

The professor told of Hon's rise as a concert pianist. When he was done, Ramonne silently applauded. "I could feel the genius in the boy when we were at the Bayon at Angkor. I didn't know how it would manifest itself."

The vampire poured the last of the bottle into the two glasses. "Now, my old friend, let's make some plans."

The professor was elated. *Here we go again!*

———

An hour before dawn, they had agreed that the professor would start the search for suitable lodging for them both. Once approved by the vampire, the usual alterations and fortifications would be made prior to occupancy.

Meanwhile, the vampire would continue his freelance work for Ping Narong while they, together, sought information on the two great mysteries—the possibility of additional vampires in Phuket, and *who* resurrected the vampire.

Who? And why?

The vampire bid the professor *adieu* and leapt off the balcony into the night. He had scant time to find a victim and feed before dawn.

The professor went back to bed, but of course, sleep would not come.

The next day, he employed a real estate agent with the strict instructions that the property needed to be a detached house, preferably with a wall around it. A basement—rare in Bangkok, a city infamous for its seasonal flooding—would be desirable. A pool was unnecessary, as were gardens, sun decks, or patios. The more private the better. Price was not really an issue, but of course he never told the agent this.

After several days of being shown the fancy residences of Thailand's elite—soap opera stars, politicians, generals—he finally saw something on Sukhumvit Soi 31 that caught his fancy.

It was the home of a former CIA agent who never left Bangkok after being made redundant. A confirmed bachelor in his early sixties, he chose to drink himself to death rather than return home to the land of the "mundane and predictable," as he referred to the USA. "There were two skills he excelled at—drinking and whoring," as the agent so delicately put it.

When Professor Kaestle took the tour, a pair of bright-pink stiletto heels were at the bottom of the staircase—apparently worn by a damsel *du jour*, who had been so shocked to wake up and find her patron dead as the proverbial doorknob, that she ran into the dawn without stopping for her shoes.

In keeping with its occupant's highly secretive past, the house was very private. A high white wall was topped with Thailand's favorite way of discouraging uninvited guests— shards of glass embedded in the mortar. A huge iron gate had been modified with a metal barricade—much like those used on castles and fortresses. It had to be manually operated, and the professor was assured that once it was secured, the property was virtually impenetrable.

There were gardens and a lawn—nothing precious, but not barren either. A shaded veranda ran around most of the first floor, and each of the bedrooms on the second floor had its own canopied balcony.

But the major selling point was the games room beneath the house. Here there was a typical "man cave"—oversize TV, bar, pool table. And at one end, a huge walk-in vault. This, the professor was told, was actually the owner's gun closet, but the arms and ammunition had been removed.

The professor could picture his master at rest in there—completely secure—surrounded by his wines and his other most precious possessions.

The vampire had given him complete autonomy in the quest for a new dwelling, and so after an obligatory round of negotiations, the property was leased and he went about the task of renovating it.

—————

Meanwhile, Ramonne continued to render his services to Ping Narong, who was delighted to have him back. If there was a task of extreme difficulty and risk, he'd send Ramonne. If there was an enemy that seemed impossible to eradicate, he'd send Ramonne.

Ping felt invincible. And his empire was growing. The weeks since Ramonne's mysterious reappearance had been the gangster's "golden days."

One night, after Ramonne had dispatched a Bulgarian gypsy swine named Django, who had attempted to renege on a deal involving over three hundred AK-47s and a dozen kilos of heroin, Ramonne and Ping left the apartment building he owned and where he did his business, and went to the Oriental Hotel.

They sat outside by the river and Ping ordered a steak. Ramonne ordered a bottle of Contador Rioja.

Once the waiter had left, Ping leaned forward. "So, Jao Nai, all is well with you...yes?"

Ramonne smiled. "Yes, Jao Phor. All is well. And thank you for your patronage. Without you, well…let's just say—"

"You owe me nothing," Ping interrupted him. "It is I who is in your debt. But I feel you are troubled. Tell me, how can I help?"

The waiter returned with the wine. He took his time uncorking it and pouring a sample for tasting. Ramonne took his time tasting it, deliberately making the man await his decision. Finally he nodded and the wine was poured.

Alone again, Ramonne leaned in to Ping. "There are two things troubling me. One, I fear, you cannot help me with."

"Yes?"

"The foul man you dispatched the evening I appeared in the pool of his blood."

Ping nodded. "Somchai Suwanaphan."

"Yes. Why him? Why then? Why there?"

Ping replied, "As you well know, our feud was ancient. We were going to go at it eventually. As to the timing, I received a warning that he would be coming after me. I went after him instead. As for where the hit occurred…well, that's where he was."

"You received a warning? From who?"

Ping leaned back in his chair while the waiter served his seared foie gras. Again he waited for him to leave before he spoke. "You know I have connections everywhere…with people who should have nothing to do with me. To be seen with me would be their ruin. But these same people allow me to continue to do what I do, as long as it benefits them. I assume it was one of these people. But, truthfully, I know no more than that."

"All right. I won't pursue it. Now, tell me about Dimitri Kirilov."

"Ah, Phuket. Did you like that? I thought you might."

"No. Actually I found it quite disturbing."

"Why?"

Ramonne pondered whether he should actually tell Ping of his suspicions. He decided against it. "It was not easy. This man —diminutive as he was—actually was very difficult to dispatch."

Ping laughed. "I know. That's why I sent you."

Ramonne was getting annoyed. "Jao Phor. You paid me a fortune. Triple the ordinary hit…Why?"

Ping pushed his empty plate aside. "Why? Because that little cunt has stolen over four million dollars in arms to Afghanistan. And he not only fucked me once; he did it twice."

"Did you go after him before?"

"Of course I did."

"And?"

"And *nothing*….My men fucking disappeared."

————

Ping left when he finished his meal. The vampire stayed behind with another bottle of wine. He thought of what he had learned when Ping was questioned by him. Nothing. Ping truly didn't know the source that led to the assassination in the alley.

The patio was dressed for Christmas, with dozens of red potted poinsettias and hundreds of tiny white lights. Ramonne allowed himself to stroll down memory lane as he finished his wine. It was in the hotel's famous Bamboo Bar in 1947 that he met Jim Thompson, the legendary silk king. World War II had just ended and, as a non-commissioned special forces agent, Thompson chose to stay in the kingdom. He formed a partnership and purchased the Oriental. Fate led Ramonne through the doors of the newly opened hotel and into the position of compère of the Bamboo Bar. This led to a long friendship and several adventures.

He turned his head towards the old Author's Wing, still standing amid the newer and remodeled buildings. A huge silver and gold Christmas tree was visible in the study. It was in the room with its historical photos of Bangkok that he first took a spellbound young Martin Larue on a vivid three-dimensional tour of the city's past.

He smiled at the memory. As he finished his wine, he placed a wad of Thai baht on the table and stood. He walked along the waterfront, lost in memories.

Suddenly an image intruded on his thoughts. He stopped dead in his tracks.

It was an image of Martin. Not the virginal lad he seduced and corrupted so long ago. No, this was the family man who joined Ramonne nine years ago to save his wife and unborn daughter from the sacrificial necromancy of Toshiro Muraki, the deranged Japanese agent. As Ramonne concentrated, the image became as clear as an IMAX projection.

Martin walked to the water's edge and leaned on the rail. He stared reflectively into the dark water. After a few moments he reached into his jacket pocket and retrieved an item wrapped in parchment. He unwrapped the parchment and revealed a pistol. He turned the gun and studied it a moment, before tossing it into the river.

The image faded as Ramonne realized what he had just witnessed. Muraki, the Black Dragon, pursued Ramonne for over half a century, in the mistaken belief that Ramonne's apparent immortality came from the Oracle. The Japanese had stolen the artifact in World War II and hidden it in the basement of the Oriental—then a Japanese military hospital.

Muraki learned to his dismay that all he was gaining when he finally possessed the Oracle was the gift of *eternal death*. Hence the sacrificial fire that was meant to restore him to normalcy. Ramonne couldn't allow this to proceed, with Martin's wife and unborn daughter as the intended victims, and had cast his own spell learned from the ancient book *The Eleusinian Mysteries and Other Pagan Rituals*, and Muraki was restored to normal mortality.

Now he knew—Martin killed Muraki. Shot him to avenge Ramonne.

Ramonne was proud of the lad. He wanted to thank him, but returned to his original promise to leave him alone. *Let him live his life.*

Ramonne was spending the days as Ping's guest in a fortified room in the apartment building Ping owned on Sukhumvit Soi 24. The windows had been painted black and boarded up, and a bronze coffin installed where the bed once stood. Ramonne didn't *need* to spend the night in a coffin, but he found it the most comfortable way for him to guarantee safe passage of the daylight hours. He locked it from within. He decided to take a ride on the network of canals that caused Bangkok to once be known as the "Venice of the East," and hailed a passing water taxi. He would hop off at some point and then take to the rooftops.

6

About twenty-four hours after her arrival, Juliette and Hon finally appeared at the apartment on Soi Langsuan. Martin and Areeya had agreed not to question or chastise them, but to welcome them instead.

Within thirty minutes, Hon apologized for leaving so soon, but he needed to go to the studio. He kissed Juliette modestly on both cheeks and left.

Once the door closed, there was a long awkward moment, which eventually little Nina broke. "I like your hair." She smiled.

Juliette smiled back. "I like yours, too."

"So, Juliette, where are you from?" Martin queried.

"The Luberon. Do you know it?"

"Yes. In Provence. Beautiful country."

"*Oui. C'est tres belle*…You have been there?"

"Yes. Many years ago. It was considered off the path then. Most tourists chose the coastal routes. Nice, Saint-Tropez."

Juliette wrinkled her nose. "Not today. *L'anglais* ruined it."

Martin raised an eyebrow. "The Brits?"

"Actually it was just one. Peter Mayle. You know who he was?"

"Yes. He wrote *A Year in Provence*. The best-selling book about his purchase and remodeling of a 200-year-old stone farmhouse in the Luberon."

"*Oui*. Now, once Easter passes the hordes start to descend. Busloads of them. The siege lasts through the summer into the fall. Only the change of weather to winter can stop them."

Martin smiled. "I was fortunate to have visited before the book. I took the proverbial break from college, to travel in Europe before my senior year. I was fortunate to wander into Ménerbes one evening. I've never forgotten how beautiful that ancient hilltop village was."

"It still is. It's just crowded."

Another awkward moment of silence was broken this time by Areeya. "Is your room alright? Do you have everything you need?"

"Yes. *C'est bon. Merci beaucoup*."

"Good…By the way, Hon never told us how you two met."

Juliette seemed to think about this a few moments before responding. "It was quite amusing, actually."

"Yes?"

"I had recently arrived in Paris. To begin a course in fashion design at Parsons Paris. My parents had arranged for me to live with an aunt in the 9th arrondissement. It is near the Opera House. I was late for school one day and I was running for the Métro, not looking where I was going. I literally ran into Hon. Knocked me right on my *derrière…Très embarrassant*. He was such a gentleman."

"Of course."

"My books and papers were scattered all over the Rue Auber, blowing in the wind. He chased them for me. Apologized profusely—even though it was completely my fault. And then I saw the poster. There were a number of them in front of the Opera. I gasped. '*C'est tu?*' Is that you…? Of course it was. He asked if I might like to go to the concert. He left my name at the box office and backstage and *voila*! That's how we met."

Martin smiled to himself. He supposed this was a regular occurrence in the handsome lad's life, and one of the perks of being a recognized musician.

Juliette had a remote control in her hand and a puzzled look on her face. "Do you have a TV?"

Martin smiled. When Areeya moved in with Martin, she had completely redecorated the bachelor flat he'd had for over ten years. They were seated in the living room. Instead of the comfortable Boxetti couch that felt like you were encased in butter, Martin and Areeya were sitting together on an Auburn sofa, and Juliette was seated in one of a pair of Roma armchairs.

Martin got up and moved to a huge neo-Grecian modular bookcase. He opened two doors, which folded back to reveal a sixty-inch Samsung flat screen.

"Watch what you like. Channel 784 is the French channel. TV Monde."

"I'm going to bed," Areeya announced.

"I'll be there shortly," he added. "Do you need anything before we leave you?"

"No. I'm fine, thank you."

"All right. *Bonsoir*."

———

Martin spent an hour on the phone in his study with various business concerns in the States that needed his attention. The twelve-hour difference between Bangkok and New York, made it mid-morning for his attorneys and bankers.

Areeya was propped up in their Tuscany sleigh bed with a half-dozen pillows, reading a Tabitha King novel, when he joined her. He picked up the Leonardo da Vinci biography he was halfway through, and they read silently for a while.

Finally Martin broke the silence. "I *like* her."

Areeya looked at him over her reading glasses. "I do too...I just don't know if we can trust her."

Martin was puzzled. "*Trust* her? With what?"

"Our son."

"Sweetheart. They're dating, not getting married."

"Not yet."

Martin was perplexed. But he had learned a long time ago not to argue with his wife. He could not win.

So he leaned over and kissed her and then went back to his book.

———

In the living room the sound from the TV covered the conversation Juliette was having on her mobile phone.

"I miss you, already."

A pause while she listened and then, "Are you sure? I won't disturb you?"

Another pause. "Yes. I understand. The doorman will call a cab for me. Moonstar Studios. Lat Phrao. Thank you, darling."

She turned the TV volume down a little, got her coat, and quietly went out the front door.

———

"It's twelve bars, the same as the intro, and then a return to the chorus—right?" John, the guitarist, was seated on a stool with his Gibson on his lap.

Hon was at the piano and seemed annoyed at the question. "No. Eight bars, *not* the same as the intro, and then a return to the chorus."

"Are you sure?"

"Yes. It's my song. I wrote the fucking thing."

John looked to Ben and Nippy, who both just shrugged.

"Once more. From the top," Hon intoned, and Nippy

counted off with his sticks.

The piece was a beautiful straight-ahead jazz composition that had a tricky opening progression that the trio had been working on for the past hour. This was extremely frustrating for all of them because once they finally were through the opening stanzas, the piece allowed them the chance to do what they really wanted to do—improvise. Hon had built in solo sections for each instrument—if they could ever just get to them.

They had just started to play, when the stage door opened and Juliette appeared.

Hon smiled and got up from the piano. Discernible groans were heard as they stopped playing and watched as Hon went and swept her into his arms.

"*Yoko's* back." John grinned and the others nodded agreement. They got up and left their instruments.

"Darling, don't let me stop your work," Juliette breathed between kisses.

Hon watched as the band grabbed cigarettes or beers and headed for the door. "Don't worry. They don't mind a break."

Hon took her by the hand and led her off to the private room that had been outfitted with a bed.

Outside, the band sat on the patio. Ben looked at his watch. "How long you figure this time?"

Nippy grinned. "Fifteen minutes?"

"And a half-hour post-coital," John added.

"Post *what*?" Ben queried.

"Cuddling."

"Christ…We've been here a week. And we've mostly been hanging around waiting for Hon."

"Relax." John lit another cigarette. "It's *his* record. We're just sidemen. We're getting paid, right?"

Ben shrugged. "Fuck it. I'm getting a beer. Anybody else?" Two hands went up and Ben went to the canteen.

Christmas was just a week away, which meant that the foreign businessmen in Bangkok were well into their long liquid lunches and office parties. Their Thai staff took the time off in stride, as a benefit to working for the *farangs*—the foreigners. They would celebrate Christmas and New Year, even though one holiday had nothing to do with their religion, and the other nothing to do with their calendar. *Their* new year celebration would come in mid-April—Songkran.

Professor Kaestle took advantage of the readily available workforce during this holiday period to turn the ex-CIA man's home into the vampire's lair. Without questioning anything, a small army of carpenters, welders, electricians, and laborers had done the transformation in record time. The final movement of the vampire's possessions from the storage vault to the house was done at night, under the vampire's supervision.

The solid mahogany coffin with bronze handles and a padded silk interior was the last piece to be moved.

This task was done with the help of just two men—a driver and someone to help with the lifting. None of the other crew had ever seen the coffin, and as far as they knew, they had just completed the renovation of a stately old house to suit the tastes of an eccentric and very rich *farang*.

After the coffin was moved and placed on a bier in the center of the former gun vault, Professor Kaestle paid the men and watched as the van pulled out of the driveway.

He heaved a heavy sigh as he saw the vampire emerge from the shadows and take to the rooftops to follow the van. He knew that by dawn both of the men would be dead and their drained corpses weighted down and sunk in the Chao Phraya River.

————

"Look, Daddy." Nina proudly displayed her new school uniform. With her hair in the regulation pigtails required of all girls at Shrewsbury International in grades one through seven, Martin thought she looked like a character in a Japanese *manga* cartoon. Adorable. "Very nice." He smiled and they rode the elevator to the lobby where he watched as she got in the BMW and On took her to school.

He paused to look at the progress on the mega-skyscraper being constructed across the street. It seemed a new floor was added every day. He shook his head in wonder and headed back upstairs.

Areeya was in the kitchen with Soon, planning the first of three dinner parties they would host at Christmas. One was Christmas Eve; one was Christmas Day; and the other was on the 29th, the day before Hon would leave for Cologne and the start of the recording sessions on January 2nd.

"Martin, they're not here."

"*Who's* not here?"

"Hon and Juliette."

"Are you sure?"

"Of course I'm sure."

"But she was here last night. I never heard Hon come in, but I assume he came home early in the morning."

"He didn't come home, and she went out."

Martin went down the hall to see for himself. The beds in both Hon's and the guest room were untouched. He looked at his watch. "Eight-thirty…Let me call the studio."

Just then the front door opened and Hon and Juliette appeared.

"*Bonjour.*"

"Good morning." Not sure what else to say, Martin followed with, "Good rehearsal?"

"*Comme ci, comme ça,*" Hon replied with the French hand waving gesture that meant not good, but not bad.

"Juliette. When did you go out?" Areeya asked.

"After you went to bed. I missed him so much and I was *très ennuyée.*"

Areeya looked puzzled. "Bored?"

Hon offered, "She was bored, so I told her I'd have Virit get a taxi to bring her to the studio…We had fun."

"But now I'm *épuisé*. Exhausted. I'm going to bed, *mon chérie*." She kissed Hon on the cheek and sauntered down the hall.

With her arms crossed, Areeya watched her go. With an arched eyebrow, she turned to Hon.

Hon just shrugged. "What?"

"It would be nice to know when you're coming and going. Since you got home we've seen very little of you. And since *her* arrival, we've barely seen you at all."

"Mom, I'm a big boy now. Don't worry about me." He hugged her to him. Try as she might not to give in, Areeya finally surrendered and hugged him back. He planted a kiss on both her cheeks and released her. "Now, I need to get some sleep. I'm due back at the studio at five-thirty."

She watched as he headed down the hall. She turned to Martin with a shocked look on her face. "He went in her room!"

Now it was Martin's turn to smile. "Of course he did."

———

Ramonne entered the vault in the basement of his new lair and admired the way the professor had arranged his most precious possessions. The Degas, the Cézanne, and the Manet in their gilt frames had been hung on bolts the workmen had driven into the thick concrete walls. Tiffany lamps, a Victorian carved oak writing desk, and a floor-to-ceiling wine rack bulging with over 200 vintage red wines.

On a Louis XIV side table, a Bang & Olufsen turntable stood at the ready. Ramonne selected an LP from a bookcase and placed the needle into the groove. Soon the sweet melodic horn of Miles Davis' "In a Silent Way" wafted through the air.

The professor was waiting patiently outside the vault's door to close it and spin the locking mechanism. His master, safely secured, would arise at dusk and open the vault himself from within.

Without looking up from the turntable, the vampire spoke very softly: "It was *you*."

"I beg your pardon, sir?"

"It was you…*You* told Ping Narong where he could ambush Somchai."

The professor made no reply. He stepped aside as the vampire walked though the vault's doorway and into his study.

"Somehow, that death, at that time and in that place, opened a portal and released me from my entrapment in a netherworld."

A book lay on a table next to a leather wingback chair. *The Eleusinian Mysteries*. It had hinges and a lock of rust-eaten iron, in the manner of books printed in Europe in the seventeenth century.

He opened the book carefully. It emitted a noxious odor of decay that rose up from the withered, stained and yellowed pages.

"This was the key to my battle with Muraki and the fire demon Rakshasa. The curses, the chants, the spiritual liberation —they are all in here."

The pages that Ramonne held open were written in an alphabet of symbols known as Vatteluttu—a Tamil script used in southern India in the fourth century A.D. It was identical in style to the symbols carved on the Oracle.

He closed the book and put it down gently. "After I studied it, the next evening it was gone. You took it, didn't you?"

The professor didn't answer, and Ramonne didn't wait."

"It took me an entire evening to crack the code and learn the chants to battle with Rakshasa. The symbols are completely indecipherable to most mere mortals. But you are not *most* mortals…are you, professor? How long did it take you to figure out how to return me to this Earth?"

The professor spoke very slowly and with a deep sigh. "Nine years."

The vampire arched an eyebrow. "Nine years?"

"I'm sorry. I—"

"Don't be sorry, old friend. Only you could have understood this." He pointed to the book. "Only you could have figured it out. I didn't see it earlier because you are not normal."

"I beg your pardon, sir?"

"You and I have been through similar transformations. I can't read your thoughts as clearly as a normal mortal."

"Good to know, sir."

"Don't get cocky. I can still bend your will to serve me…Not that I intend to."

"Of course not."

The professor was holding a bottle of red wine, and the vampire took it from him.

"A Château Lafite Rothschild. Are we celebrating?"

"Call it a 'homecoming.' It's good to have you back, sir."

"It's good to *be* back. Who was it who said, 'It's good to be *anywhere*'?"

"I believe that was Keith Richards, sir."

"Oh yes. The rock star who refuses to die."

The professor uncorked the bottle and decanted it. He waited while the vampire tasted it.

"Please, have a glass with me."

"If you insist, sir."

"I do."

Ramonne poured a generous glass of the 3,000-dollar wine and leaned back in his chair. "Now tell me, old friend, once you figured out that I could be brought back, how did you make it happen?"

The professor sat opposite the vampire. "The text was clear…Well, actually, it took about four years before it was somewhat clear. What it said was basically: Evil must replace evil. In other words, it would take the sacrifice of a truly evil person to substitute for one taken off this mortal coil by a demon such as Rakshasa."

Ramonne looked directly at the professor. "Really? *That's* what it says? Evil must replace evil?"

"Yes."

Ramonne studied the trails the rich wine left on the side of his glass. "The chants that I learned...'*O Fire, I seek the truth of knowledge. Hear me, for I am the Priest of the Call.*' Etcetera. Ultimately they were failing and the fire beast was about to take Martin's wife and her unborn daughter. That meant it would have taken someone pure and innocent."

"But it didn't. You gave up yourself to save them."

Ramonne remembered the words: "*I approach thee with outstretched hands and with obeisance...With a mind strong for sacrifice, I beseech thee—*"

Professor Kaestle finished the plea: "Take me. And it did. It took you."

The vampire was quiet for a few moments, mulling this over.

"What did you do next?"

"I applied a system of checks and balances to everything you had done from the moment I met you."

"Really?"

"Yes. I decided that when you...excuse me...when you 'fed,' you did so out of necessity and you chose your victims selectively."

Ramonne sipped his wine and gave a little nod. "Yes. And?"

"You preyed upon the dregs of society—the thugs, the corrupt, the sick with little time left."

Ramonne nodded. "Yes, occasionally. Go on."

"I played the odds. I decided that the time that counted in this equation was when Muraki and his Oracle entered your life."

"Nineteen forty-seven."

"Yes. You had basically adapted a 'culling' attitude to your choice of victims, and, when you could, you took out extremely vicious, violent, evil persons. Or, even worse, Black Dragon agents who called on a twenty-foot fire-breathing devil for their salvation."

Ramonne didn't move. He sat in the wing-backed chair as stiff as an Egyptian mummy and stared at the professor.

Five minutes went by. Neither of them moved or spoke.

Finally Ramonne broke the silence: "Next?"

"Next I went looking for an alternative."

"An *alternative*?"

"For you."

"Of course."

"I found what I was looking for on the Internet."

"On the *what*?"

"I'm sorry. I realize you paid no attention before, but that 'gizmo' as you used to refer to it, is now very popular. If you want information—that's where you go to get it."

"The Internet?"

"Yes. There's a criminal database for Thailand, and one name stood out from the rest."

"Somchai Suwanaphan."

"Yes."

"Why him? What did he do?"

"You name it. His family were Chinese mafia. Migrated to Thailand in the mid-nineteenth century."

"As did I," Ramonne reflected.

"I realize that. Somchai was born a *jao phor*—a Godfather. His father was killed when he was still a teenager, and he took over the largest mafia syndicate in Thailand without protest in 1971. Their international operations included drug distribution, human trafficking, extortion, and abduction. At home they added illegal gambling, protection, prostitution, drug production, and smuggling."

Ramonne sipped his wine while he considered this.

"He sounds like a common gangster. Nothing special."

"Apparently he was—at first. But because of his young age, he was perceived as weak. He soon began to be challenged. So he decided to make his enemies fear him. He mercilessly killed anyone he even suspected of cheating or challenging him. And the deaths he devised were horrific. He didn't shoot his enemies —he butchered them. He constructed elaborate cells and torture chambers, and carried out weekly executions."

Whether Ramonne was impressed or appalled couldn't be known. He was impassive.

"He was soon known as 'Petchakat.' Do you know what it means in Thai?"

Ramonne waited.

"Executioner. He was called the 'Executioner.'"

"Apt."

"I think so."

"Next?"

"Next, I did the math."

"The *math*?"

"Yes. If you had been active for those forty years—1971 to 2011—you would probably have sent four thousand mortal souls to their graves. But you were withdrawn from action, so to speak, on two different occasions—which probably saved a thousand or more. And you were in—as you describe it—a netherworld these past nine years."

Ramonne continued to seem more interested in the wine than the professor's discourse.

"As I said earlier, I don't think a majority of your kills were unjustified. So I will give you the benefit of the doubt and say you killed a couple thousand innocents in that period."

"How kind of you."

"I detect sarcasm…but I'll continue. Now, let's look at Somchai. He took over the family business in the early 1970s. By 2019, the CIA believed he was responsible for the brutal murder of fifteen hundred or more of his colleagues. This didn't seem to bother anyone very much. But there is the matter of close to a thousand human trafficking victims. Boats sinking, gang wars. And another several hundred in their new venture—terrorism. They now contract to blow up hotels, shoot up resorts, and bring down airplanes for a fee."

This got Ramonne's attention.

"So, as I said, I did the math. I figured if it truly took evil to replace evil…well it was a good bet that Somchai Suwanaphan was more evil than you."

"I'm not sure if I should be flattered or not."

"There was more of interest on the criminal database. There was a list of known associates of Petchakat. They were divided into cohorts and rivals. On the rivals list was Apinya Channarong."

"Ping Narong."

"Yes."

"And so you thought you had your target for the exchange and the assassin."

"Yes."

"What did you do?"

"I thought…What would you do? I knew about Ping of course."

"Of course, but you had no direct contact with him."

"No, but *you* did. In your desk was a notebook. There was one phone number in it. I knew it was Ping. Who else could it be?"

"Presumptuous. But correct."

"By now, their rivalry was actually common knowledge. It was in the newspapers and on TV. It was legendary."

"Really? I *have* been gone a long time."

"Anyway, I decided the best way to get to Somchai was to become a customer."

"A *customer*?"

"Yes. I invented a character. An eccentric multi-millionaire with an expensive drug habit."

"*You?*" Ramonne started to laugh, but the professor cut him off.

"Yes. Me. It's quite interesting what money can buy you."

"*My* money."

"Yes. Your money. I acquired a Mercedes and a driver. It took about six months of dealing with petty street scum, but as I kept increasing the amount I purchased, I was soon assured that I was now dealing with Somchai's people. I never saw the man himself, of course."

"You did all this…for me?"

"Yes. Of course…Anyway, after another six months or so, I played my hand. I placed an order so lucrative—"

"Might I ask what you were willing to spend?"

"Two million dollars."

"*Two million dollars?*"

"Yes. But I stipulated that Somchai himself must be at the exchange, and that I would set the time and place. He could bring his bodyguards. He could bring an army. But he had to come in person."

"I can't believe you're still alive."

"I wasn't sure I'd make it through, but I had to try. Anyway, the book had many stipulations on how to perform the exchange. A most particular one was that the target's assassination had to take place in a holy shadow's peak."

"A holy shadow?"

"Yes. Eventually I found an alley behind a Buddhist temple where the full moon cast a massive shadow. I decided that was where the drug deal had to take place. The 'peak' I took to mean midnight."

"Of course."

"Once it was set, I called Ping. I gave him enough information that he knew I was connected in some way, and he believed what I told him. I gave him the time and place where he could find Somchai. I said he would be guarded, but that he was expecting to make a quick exchange, and I doubted he had given the occurrence much thought, even though it involved two million dollars."

"My two million dollars," Ramonne repeated.

"Yes...*your* two million dollars. The time came and we pulled the Mercedes into the entrance to the alley. I had the car armor-plated as a precaution, but it turned out not to be necessary. I sat in the car with the money, the *book*, and a very nervous driver. The first of Somchai's men arrived right at midnight, and I started the chant.

"*Oh venerable Goddess, source of life...hear me, for I am the Priest of the Call...T'is thine in Earth's profundities to dwell...Fast by the wide and dismal gates of hell...*

"In total he brought four men. They stepped into the alley as I sat in the car and continued to chant.

"*To wretched mortals thy power is known...Bring forward the vast and supreme word...*

"Finally Somchai stepped into the alley. He was looking at his phone, like people do now almost non-stop, so he didn't—"

"Why was he looking at his phone?"

"I'll explain later. Just know that very few people actually talk on them anymore. Anyway, he never saw Ping Narong and his men when they stepped out of the shadows. I continued to chant while Somchai was gunned down.

"*Hear my call. I offer thee the sacrificat of the rite—*"

"He was on his phone?"

"Yes. That's not important. Ping's men disarmed Somchai's goons and let them go. I finished the chant.

"*From thine the task, according to thy will...Life to produce and all that lives to kill...*

"The driver started the car and we drove away without seeing whether it worked or not."

"That's insane."

Ramonne poured the rest of the expensive bottle into their glasses.

7
———

Music is magical.

This thought occupied Martin's subconscious as he listened to the blending of four separate instruments into one magnificent sound, weaving a tapestry that alternated between harmony and solo, seamlessly. Finally the piece began to draw to a close as the dominant sound of the piano brought it back to where it had started. In an incredible mad flurry that seemed like it would never end...it gradually faded as each instrument stopped playing until finally it was just the piano—Hon's magical piano—and then that, too, faded and stopped.

Martin realized he'd been holding his breath. He stood in the glassed-in balcony over the soundstage. He had arrived, unannounced, shortly after midnight, and was led up to the viewing area. He looked at his watch. The piece he had just observed them perform had lasted over twenty minutes.

He knew his son was a genius. He'd seen that proven to him time and time again. But he had never seen anything like this in his life. Tears were forming. Tears of joy.

Downstairs, the musicians had left their instruments for a break. He didn't see Hon. He turned to go down—and there he was.

75

"Hey. They told me you were here. What's up?"

Martin was unable to speak. He pulled the boy to him and hugged him. Hon did not resist, and Martin could feel the strength in his young arms.

"Dad…? Are you okay?"

They broke the embrace and Martin wiped the moisture from his eyes.

"Yes. I'm fine…That piece you just played—is that yours?"

"Yes. I call it 'Tonle Sap Sonata.' After the—"

"The lake in Cambodia. We went camping there when you were just ten."

"Did you like it?"

"It's beautiful."

Hon went to a refrigerator and got a bottle of water. He offered one to Martin, who declined. He sat on the couch and Martin followed.

They sat in silence a few moments. Finally Martin spoke. "Hon, you know how much we love you."

The young man nodded. "Of course."

"From the moment we saw you—"

"In a dump outside Phnom Penh, scavenging for food and bits of scrap metal to sell."

"We loved you then. But you were a wild thing."

"So were you. A mad *barang* who wanted to adopt a dozen scruffy street orphans."

Martin laughed. "Sixteen street orphans to be precise. And technically we didn't adopt *them*. We formed the orphanage as a home for them. But *you*…you we *did* adopt. And we have loved you as if you were born to us."

"I know that. And I love you and mom, too. Always have. Always will."

Martin smiled. "We have been so close. Such a tight family. And we couldn't be prouder of you. You have a gift that you share with the world and bring great joy."

Hon leaned back and listened.

"But your mother is afraid that we are losing you. She fears that you will forget us."

"That will never happen."

"She's afraid it's happening already."

"*What*...? Why?"

Martin swallowed. "Juliette...She thinks you're spending too much time with her."

As if she had just been cued, Juliette entered the room. Her hair was uncombed and she had puffy eyes. She stifled a yawn.

"Hey." Hon pulled her to him.

She curled up on the couch and rested her head on Hon's shoulder and looked at Martin.

An awkward silence was broken by the appearance of Ju, the stage manager. "Hon. Do you want to keep the same set-up?"

"No. Thanks. Set it up for the next track. 'Prelude to a Kiss.' I'll be down in a moment."

Ju nodded and left.

Juliette smiled. "'Prelude to a Kiss.' I like that."

Martin shifted in his seat, suddenly feeling uncomfortable. He wanted to continue the conversation, but didn't know how. "I should be going."

As Martin got up, Hon disentangled himself from Juliette and stood. He put his hands on Martin's shoulders. "Don't worry. Okay...? Tell mom there's nothing to worry about. I'm just busy. But it won't always be like this."

Martin smiled and they hugged again briefly. As Martin went out the door, he saw Juliette smiling at him.

The coldness of the smile sent a shudder through him.

———

Midnight found Ramonne in a private club just off Bangkok's crowded nighttime mecca of Sukhumvit Soi 11. The club had a distinctly Latin feel to it, with bartenders in tight dinner jackets and the waitresses in floral Spanish dresses. Male patrons were encouraged to wear a Panama hat from the ready supply by the front door.

The Havana Club was a real speakeasy, with no exterior signage. To gain entrance, one stepped into an old-fashioned telephone booth and punched in a seven-digit code that was changed regularly.

Most of the customers drank mojitos, and a few of the men smoked cigars.

Ramonne sat in a corner with a bottle of Rioja. He was here not for his own amusement, but on assignment for Ping Narong.

At precisely 1:15, a young Thai in a John Varvatos suit entered, accompanied by two young, overly made-up girls in tight-fitting dresses with low-cut tops. A velvet rope was stretched across a staircase. One of the bartenders smiled and, with a slight bow, opened the rope to let the young man and his small harem ascend the stairs.

The vampire waited a few moments, and then he too approached the stairs. The bartender made no move to open the rope. Not, that is, until Ramonne merely looked at him. Then, like a man in a trance, he unhooked the rope.

At the top of the stairs was an old wooden door, much like that on a ship's galley. Ramonne tried the knob. It opened and he stepped onto the rooftop.

A small crowd was gathered there. Couches, old lanterns, and low tables were arranged in groups. The music from below was piped in through small speakers.

The young man Ramonne sought was seated on a couch at the edge of the roof, overlooking the busy street below. Instead of mojitos, a bucket was on the table and a waiter was uncorking a bottle of Moët & Chandon champagne.

Ramonne waited until the waiter left and the trio hoisted their glasses, before approaching.

"Chakra Boonksukol...Or would you prefer I call you 'Sharky'?"

The young man looked up. "Who the fuck are you?"

Ramonne didn't answer. Instead he just looked at the two girls. Without a word, they put their drinks down and left.

"Hey! *Yet mai!*" he shouted as they went through the door.

Ramonne pulled a chair up and sat opposite Chakra.

"You know why I'm here, don't you?"

"I have no fucking idea who the fuck you are."

"It doesn't matter who I am. What matters is your *debt*."

"My debt...? What the fuck are you talking about?"

"I think the Thai word is *tid khang*. Your *tid khang* to my boss is a lot of money."

"Your boss? Who is your *boss*?"

"Ping Narong."

Now, for the first time, real fear appeared in Chakra's eyes. But the gangster bravado that had been instilled in him still denied it.

"Ping Narong!" he spat. "That *hee-ah*. The old man is finished. Everyone knows that."

Ramonne smiled. "That *old man* sent me here to collect thirty million Thai baht."

"Thirty million baht? He's *baa*. I admit to a small debt—ten million baht. I can pay half of that right now."

He reached in his suit. Ramonne's hand was on his wrist before he knew it.

"There are people here...you do *not* want to be seen with a gun in Bangkok. You are not *that* important."

Ramonne tightened his grip on Chakra's wrist. Like a vise it crushed the bone.

He started to scream, but Ramonne put his other hand over his mouth.

"This is what you will do...After your visit to the hospital to get your broken wrist splinted, you will take the money—thirty million baht—and deliver it to Ping Narong before the sun goes down tomorrow evening. If not, you will not live to see another sunrise. Do you understand?"

Chakra nodded.

Ramonne released his grip and stood. Suddenly he was hungry...and the night was still young.

————

"Something foul is afoot in Phuket?"

Colin McGavin had just arrived and barely sat down when Martin quoted the note he'd found in the file Prakasan had loaned him.

"Jeez. No 'Hello, good to see you...have a drink'?"

"What would you like?"

Colin motioned at Martin's wine glass. "What's that?"

"A Schiopetto Pinot Grigio...Very nice." He waved at Sand, the waiter. "Bring a bottle, please."

Colin picked up the menu. Martin put his hand over it. "We'll have time for that. I want to know what you meant."

Colin put the menu down. "Whatever happened to reporter's privilege? Why were you reading that file?"

"I was curious. Something you told me sounded strange."

"The whole trip was strange. That note was just a thought I had when I was in the bar, thinking about what I'd write for the *Times*. I thought I threw it away...Turned out I didn't write anything."

They were seated on the second floor of No Idea, a gastropub on Sukhumvit Soi 22. It was lunchtime and the downstairs area was filled with expat businessmen. The second floor was quiet and private.

"Tell me what happened."

"I told you about the incinerated body at the temple. But there were other weird things." Colin leaned in. "There are all these Russians around. Especially in places like Andara. The GM told me some of them show up with a million dollars or more in cash, which they want stored in the resort's safe…There are boats coming and going into small private headlands, and large plastic garbage bags are being transferred. Sometimes to a ship, sometimes to shore. And people are disappearing…a lot."

"Did you tell Prakasan this?"

"No. Of course not. He'd assign me to go undercover and find out what's going on."

The waiter arrived with the wine. He opened it. Martin tasted it and nodded. After it was poured, Martin leaned in to Colin.

"You're a reporter. Isn't that what you do?"

"No. That's how you get killed. I'm a writer—fiction mostly. You know that. *Sometimes* I'm a journalist. I cover local politics, festivals, lunar eclipses…stuff like that." He drained his wine glass in one swallow. "Mmm, that *is* good." He refilled his glass.

"Glad you like it."

"Can we order now?"

Martin smiled. "Not just yet." He handed a thin envelope to Colin.

"There's a name in here. And some other information. All I have. It's not much. I want you to find out whatever you can. Use your resources. I'll pay whatever it takes."

Colin opened the envelope and took out the single sheet of paper. "You're right—this isn't very much."

Martin arched an eyebrow. "And?"

"I'll do what I can." He put the envelope in his pocket. "Now, can we order?"

8

Christmas Eve

Noon, and the Larue household was already buzzing with activity. Martin and Nina were decorating the three-meter real fir tree that was centered in the living room. The upscale Villa Market near Sukhumvit Soi 33 stocked a half-dozen each year at the outrageous price of 10,000 baht, over 300 dollars, and Martin had placed his order in October. Nina was tossing the tinsel while Martin was carefully placing the dozen hand-blown glass ornaments that had been in the Larue family for sixty or seventy years.

Areeya was in the kitchen with Soon and two professional chefs, preparing for tonight's *soirée*. Their guests would be arriving after six o'clock for cocktails and dinner. The menu was elaborate. Three main courses. A glazed ham, amped up a notch with a bit of dry mustard and black pepper. Roast beef with slow-cooked tomatoes and garlic. And, of course, a roast turkey with garlic, sage, and lemon.

One of the two chefs was in charge of the appetizers and side dishes, which were actually more complicated than the main courses. The appetizers included caramelized onion tarts with apple, fondue with an assortment of dippers, and pears with blue cheese and prosciutto. The sides were tender greens with champagne vinaigrette, broccoli with toasted garlic and hazelnuts, roasted Brussels sprouts with pecans, glazed carrots, green beans with pine nuts, and sour-cream mashed potatoes.

The desserts were bread pudding with fruit compôte, sour-cream apple crumb pie, and apricot parfait.

Areeya herself concentrated on the drinks. There was traditional egg nog with Plantation rum, and pomegranate ginger palomas—a tequila cocktail—offered alongside mimosas as the guests arrived. Wine would be served with the dinner.

There would be a dozen at the table: Martin and Areeya, Nina, Nina's best friend Noi and her parents, Martin's lawyer Ben and his actress wife Krystal, Hon and Juliette, and Hon's best friend Tan—a filmmaker—and his girlfriend.

The doorbell rang. Martin opened it and Virit the doorman was there with a little girl.

"Hello, Noi." Martin smiled. The girl put her hands together in the traditional Thai greeting and gave a slight bow to Martin. Nina ran up to her friend and took her hand.

"Can we play in my room?"

"Of course. But remember you promised to help Soon set the table."

"We will." And the girls disappeared.

Virit turned to leave when Martin stopped him. "Wait a minute please." Martin went to the console table and removed an envelope. "Merry Christmas." Virit smiled, and gave a slight bow. "Thank you, Khun Martin."

He closed the door and Martin shut the drawer in the table. There were several more little envelopes in it. Martin had learned a long time ago that any Thai working for him in any capacity would much prefer a cash present than a luxury item that he or she would then have to convert to cash after, no doubt, a hefty commission.

Martin went back to decorating the tree. When he finished,

he stood back to admire his handiwork. Areeya joined him. "Beautiful."

"Yes, it is." He put his arms around Areeya's waist. "The whole house is beautiful. As are you."

She turned to look up at him, and they kissed. In the kitchen, Soon smiled and the two chefs pretended not to see this romantic display.

"I'm going to put the presents under the tree." Martin released Areeya and she went back to the kitchen. He smiled as he watched her. Sixteen years later and he still loved her.

But it was hardly love at first sight.

When he met her, she was the spoiled-brat daughter of a big crooked cop, Lieutenant Colonel Boonsong of the Bang Rak police. Her nickname was "Yaya" and she was well into drugs and dangerous men. Martin didn't really know she existed until Ramonne kidnapped her as a way to lure her father and kill him.

Martin and Yaya ended up together briefly at the end of that adventure, but then they both suffered PST and it wasn't until a year later that they met again. Martin spent that year in a monastery up north, and Areeya went into rehab.

They joined forces with Ramonne to thwart a terrorist bombing in the crowded entertainment plaza of Patpong. Along the way, they fell in love.

Within a year they were married and living in Siem Reap, on the edge of the temples of Angkor. They supervised the construction of a small orphanage. The love and attention that Martin, Areeya, and their small staff showered upon those children worked miracles, and École Des Orphelins d'Angkor was soon an idyllic refuge.

"Honey…? Is everything all right?"

Martin suddenly realized he was standing immobile in front of the tree and grinning like an idiot. "Yes…Yes, of course."

Without turning to her, he wiped a few tears of joy off his cheeks and headed down the hall to fetch the presents.

In the back of the Mercedes, Hon rested his head on Juliette's shoulder. She stroked his hair while looking out the window at the slow-moving sea of traffic. "*Pourquoi*? Why do we have to go there?"

"Because…" Hon sighed. "It's Christmas Eve."

"*Christmas*. How stupid. Tell me, which fairy tale do you celebrate—Jesus or Santa Claus?"

Hon looked up at her. *Who is this woman?* he wondered.

"My dad being an American, means Christmas is celebrated no matter what your religion. It's a time for family to get together."

He propped himself on one elbow. "Truthfully, I knew nothing of religion until my dad adopted the group of us. I'm sure I was born a Buddhist, but I was passed around a lot, and religion wasn't a part of my life. When my dad took us into his orphanage, he said we could choose—Buddhism, Christianity, or nothing at all."

She frowned. "No Jews in the orphanage?"

"No…none on the staff."

"So what did you choose?"

"Buddhism. My dad was basically an atheist before he came to Thailand, but for some reason he spent a year in a monastery before coming to Siem Reap. My mom, of course, was born Buddhist."

"Are you a good Buddhist, Hon?"

"I strive for enlightenment and self-discipline. I meditate daily. But that's about it." He turned to look up at her. "What about you? The French seem to be very orthodox Christians."

"I'm not *orthodox* anything. But I do *masturbate* daily." She laughed.

"I'm not surprised. You're insatiable." They kissed. She began unbuttoning his shirt when he stopped her.

"No. We're almost there."

"Then tell him to go around the block. In Bangkok that ought to take at least an hour. Plenty of time."

"No, Juliette. We can't be late tonight."

She shook off his arms and reached for her purse. She took out a small cut-glass bottle.

"Juliette. Please. Not now."

"Why not now?"

She unscrewed the top and it held a little spoon, which she deftly dipped into the bottle. Withdrawing it, she quickly snorted the white powder. She repeated this with the other nostril.

She leaned back with a smile and sighed. Then she offered the bottle to Hon.

"No."

She sighed again.

"You're fucking boring. You know that?" She unscrewed the bottle top and snorted again.

Hon glared at her, wondering again, *Who is this woman?*

―――――

The first guests were Ben and Krystal. The attorney and his wife arrived at six o'clock sharp. Areeya greeted them with a *wai* to Ben and a kiss on the cheek and a hug for Krystal. Ben took the pomegranate drink while his wife chose a mimosa.

Martin pointed out that Krystal was standing under a mistletoe sprig. Ben moved in for a kiss when she dodged him and kissed Martin instead.

"That'll cost you," Ben huffed with a smile. "Your rates couldn't get any higher, so I'm not worried," Martin countered.

The doorbell rang and Noi's parents were next. Noi's father, Thomas, worked at the US Consulate. His wife Nan was a dark-skinned, pure-blooded Isaan beauty. Noi left the game she was playing with Nina to hug her long legs.

"Oh my God, Thomas…look at the tree."

Martin beamed with pride.

"Villa Market?" Thomas asked.

Martin nodded.

"Must have cost a fortune."

Martin shrugged. "It's Christmas."

"That it is." Thomas and Martin both took mimosas from a tray and clinked glasses. "*Chok dee,*" they said in unison.

Martin motioned to Noi. "Come here, Noi. I think there's something for you under the tree."

"Really?" Her dark-brown eyes opened wide as she followed Martin.

The base of the tree was now surrounded by presents. All shapes and sizes. All elaborately wrapped and festooned with gold and silver bows. Martin picked up a box that was almost the size of Noi, and handed it to her.

She looked at Thomas. "Can I open it now?"

Thomas looked to Krystal. She nodded. "Of course, honey."

Within seconds the wrapping had been destroyed. She turned the box until she found the flaps to open it. She reached inside and pulled out an adorable, almost life-size, plush penguin doll. Immediately, Noi crushed the fluffy doll to her.

"Noi. Look again in the box," Martin prompted. Puzzled, and without letting go of the penguin, Noi looked back inside. Immediately she beamed ear to ear. "It's a baby," she cried. She pulled the little chick out, and Martin showed her how two pieces of Velcro would allow the mother to hold her chick between her legs.

"Thank you. I love it!" She wrapped her arms around Martin's legs and hugged him. Martin smiled and patted her little head. "You're very welcome, Noi. And Merry Christmas."

While Nina was hugging Martin's legs, Thomas tapped him on the shoulder and pointed. He turned and saw his own daughter standing with her arms crossed and staring daggers at him.

He gently released himself from Noi's grip and approached

Nina. "Honey?" She turned her back on him, still keeping her arms crossed. He approached the pile of presents beneath the tree and found a box of similar dimensions as the one he gave Noi. "Nina...I believe this one is for you."

Now she unfolded her arms. "Really?" She ran and snatched it from him. She tore the wrapping and ripped open the box. Inside was another adorable little animal. This was a chubby mother wolf and her pup. Again, the pup was meant to cuddle between its mother's legs.

"Dad, thank you." She hugged his legs quickly and then took her wolf and cub to go and play with Noi and her penguins.

Before they left the room, she turned back. "But I will get some more presents tomorrow...right?"

Martin nodded his head. "Yes. Santa will bring them tonight."

Secure that her Christmas joy wasn't over, she headed off with Noi and their menagerie.

Ben had joined them by now, and he clinked glasses with Martin. "Well played. When we have a kid, I hope I'm as diplomatic."

"Never let them be jealous. They can sulk for hours. Days even. Thomas knows. Right?"

"Noi once wouldn't speak to me for two days because her friend got one of those electric scooter things that are all the rage. Her friend is only fourteen."

"Those things are insane. On our last trip to Europe they were everywhere," Martin chimed in.

"And they work well in some places, but Bangkok? Talk about a death wish."

"Actually our firm has a case involving an electric scooter," Ben remarked. "A German kid rented one on Sukhumvit and got three blocks before being hit."

"You're suing the driver?"

"Yes. The kid was actually doing the right thing. The light

was green for him. But the driver didn't see him and made a left turn right into him."

"Is he badly hurt?"

"He'll recover. But he'll be wearing casts on an arm and a leg for months, and then a long bit of physical therapy."

"Who was the driver?"

"A sixty-year-old man—a professional driver. It was a black Mercedes, and the lady of the house was in the back seat."

"At least they have money. The kid should be taken care of."

"You think? Remember 'This Is Thailand…? T-I-T' Or 'Amazing Thailand?' The family is refusing to pay anything. They claim the kid was a hazard and should be locked up."

Martin frowned. "But you'll prevail. Right?"

"I don't know. It's going to be a fight."

"What about the police? Surely they're involved."

"Oh yes. They've locked up the man who was driving. And so far the court is saying that is the extent of the liability."

"What about the insurance company?"

"Yeah. You'd think this would be a slam dunk. But they've decided to go with the 'unwarranted hazard' defense."

"I don't get it? What's the point?"

"Martin. You're very wealthy. *Hell*, let's say it—you're rich. If this happened to you, you'd no doubt go out of your way to make sure the boy was taken care of. That's the *right* thing to do. But there are people here—and everywhere—who acquired their money on the backs of others. Land schemes, embezzlement, trafficking, and some who have both legitimate and illegal ventures that have made them rich beyond imagination. These people don't kowtow to anybody. They're not going to care about a peasant like this German boy. And worst of all—they are virtually unreachable. The courts protect them."

As they all pondered this, the door opened and Hon and Juliette entered.

"Ah. The guests of honor," Martin greeted them.

Juliette had a stranglehold on Hon's arm until she saw the sprig of mistletoe.

"Ahhh. *Du'gui*." She immediately locked lips with Hon in a passionate embrace. The other guests froze and watched the spectacle as the couple finally came up for air.

"Okay…Everyone, this is Juliette. Juliette, this is everyone," Martin vamped.

"*Enchanté*." She smiled while still holding on to Hon.

"Hon. You remember Ben and Krystal?"

"Of course." Hon freed himself from Juliette's grasp, and shook Ben's hand and kissed Krystal lightly on the cheek.

"And this is Thomas and Nan. Nan's daughter Noi is in school with Nina." Juliette was already looking bored as Hon greeted them politely.

"Where's Tata?" Hon looked around.

Areeya smiled. Ever since Hon learned of her nickname Yaya, he had taken to calling his grandmother "Tata"—after a famous Thai pop singer.

"Rose and my aunts will be here tomorrow. Tonight is for friends. And *family*, of course."

As if on cue, the doorbell rang. Martin opened it. A handsome young Thai man and a beautiful Thai girl entered.

"Tan." Hon grinned and the two men embraced. "Great to see you, man."

"You too, brother."

"And who's this?"

"This is Katy."

"Katy. This is Juliette."

Juliette was sizing Tan up. She seemed to like what she saw. Without taking her eyes off of Tan, she said, "Charmed, I'm sure."

"Well, that's a full house," Martin said. "Everyone have some of Areeya's famous welcoming drinks, and we'll make our way to the dinner table."

The dinner was spectacular. The ham and the turkey were devoured. The roast beef suffered less dramatically, and Areeya figured it would be good for a few sandwiches later in the week.

Ben had brought a bottle of Australian white wine, and Martin provided both red and white wines from South Africa. By the time dessert was served, they all were definitely in a mellow mood.

Juliette was noticeably a bit more than mellow. All could tell that she was drunk. But no one seemed to mind, and the conversation basically avoided her.

However, Juliette was not to be ignored. She had a comment on every subject, whether her opinion was sought or not. Hon did his best to control her, but she was uncontrollable.

"So, Ben. Tell me, is Krystal as delicious as she looks?"

Ben turned a gentlemanly cheek, but Krystal started to get out of her chair. Ben held her arm and, reluctantly, she remained seated.

Whatever had been the topic of discussion was forgotten. Martin tried to carry on. "Have you been to Icon Siam? I'm not sure who to believe. It's either the greatest architectural achievement in Bangkok's dubious history in that field, or the worst of what it is that makes Bangkok memorable."

Nan was the first to reply. "It's fun. You have all your shops, and you're right on the river. In an amazing ethereal playground."

Areeya was next. "Yes. I agree with all that. But is our riverside experience today nothing but extravagant shopping centers? Not so long ago, the riverside was not an attractive place to live. The poor lived there. Except for the Oriental Hotel, there wasn't much reason to go to the riverside. That and the floating markets."

"And then in the mid-eighties new luxury hotels—the

Shangri La, The Sheraton—started to appear," Martin chimed in. "And next came the River City complex."

"And the history of the city began to disappear. I'm not sure this 'bigger is always better' idea is good for Bangkok."

There was silence when Areeya finished.

Nan was about to say something when, slowly, Juliette started to clap.

Puzzled, Areeya looked at her.

Finally Juliette stopped. "*C'est du vent*! Very nice. Very, very nice. Poor little rich girl, married to a man way beyond her means—concerned about a city's past being paved over to make way for massive shopping malls. *La connerie*. What bullshit. What do you do with your life except shop in expensive shopping malls?"

This outburst was followed by even more silence.

Areeya tried to ignore what had happened. "Juliette, would you like some coffee?"

"No, *merci beaucoup*. Just some more wine." She slid her half-full glass forward, slopping the red wine onto the linen table cloth.

Hon reached for the glass and she slapped him.

Hon stood and pulled Juliette's chair out from the table.

"Please excuse us." He took Juliette's hand and forced her to her feet.

"Let go of me." Juliette fought to get free of his grip.

Hon, though not much taller than Juliette, was a very strong young man, and he easily forced her from the chair and onto her feet.

"Hon?" Martin questioned.

"It's okay, Dad. She just needs some air."

Juliette struggled but Hon managed to get her out the door and into the elevator. He released his grip on her. She pulled as far away from him as she could. "What's wrong with you?" Hon said.

"*Me*…? Me? What's wrong with you?"

"I wasn't the one making a scene. Why do you always have to go too far?"

"They are a bunch of pompous assholes. *Connard*. All of them. *Je m'en fous*. I really don't give a fuck."

"They're my family. And friends."

"Then you, too. You're an asshole. *En trou du cul*."

They reached the ground floor and the door opened. Hon walked out of the cab but Juliette stayed pressed into the corner. Sulking. The door started to close and Hon put his hand in its way and it opened again. He stood in the doorway, his hand extended.

"Come on, Juliette. Let's take a walk. Get some fresh air."

"Fresh air in Bangkok? *Casse toi*. Fuck off."

She pulled a cigarette from her pocket and lit it.

"Sir. Is everything all right?" Virit the doorman was now standing behind Hon.

Hon was embarrassed and motioned again for Juliette to come out of the elevator. But she stayed in the corner, smoking and fuming.

"Master Hon, she can't smoke in the elevator."

"I know that. I'm trying to get her to come out."

"Let me try, sir. Usually the uniform does the trick."

Hon gladly stepped aside. Virit stepped into the open doorway.

"Miss. You can't smoke in the elevator. Please come out and you can smoke outside the lobby."

Juliette calmly closed her right hand with only the middle finger extended, and aimed it right at Virit.

"All right. That's enough. Virit, keep the door open." Hon went back into the cab, grabbed Juliette's right hand, and pulled. She in turn quickly stuck the cigarette in her mouth and grabbed the safety bar in the back of the cab. Hon pulled and she held on. "Damn it, Juliette. Let go."

"*Non*. You let go."

Finally Hon let his hand off her right wrist and slid it up so he wedged it behind her upper arm. Then he did the same with her left arm. The pressure on both arms caused her to let go and he was able to back her out of the cab.

"Very good, sir."

"Open the lobby door."

"Yes. Of course."

This turned out to be unnecessary as, by now, Nong, the security guard, was standing in the open lobby door wondering what was going on.

"Master Hon, is everything all right?"

"Yes, Khun Nong. Everything's fine. Just going for a little walk."

Hon dragged the girl, kicking and cursing, out the lobby door and down the steps to the garden path that led to the street, Soi Langsuan.

"Hon. Stop it. You're hurting me."

Hon immediately released his hold on her.

She rubbed her wrist while looking around. "Fuck. I dropped my cigarette."

"You know I don't like you smoking around me."

"I really don't give a shit." She pulled out the pack. "*Merde*. That was the last one."

"Good…Why don't you quit?"

"Why don't you go fuck yourself?"

They reached the main street. Across from their apartment complex the massive construction site was operating in full gear. Bare bulbs were strung on the top floor, where a massive crane was lifting stacks of concrete columns from a working base on the sixth floor.

Hon put a hand on Juliette's shoulder but she shrugged it off.

"Juliette. There's no point to this. It's Christmas Eve."

"Fuck Christmas. I didn't want to be there and you knew it. You dragged me…Why don't we just go back to the Emporium Suites? Just you and me."

"I can't do that. That's my family."

"Well it's not *my* family." Without looking, she stepped into the street. She just missed being hit by a taxi. The driver leaned on his horn.

"Juliette!"

She made it to the other side and started walking north in front of the construction site.

"Juliette. Stop. Where are you going?"

She made no response. She continued to walk up the street, heading for the skytrain station at the top of the *soi*.

"Fuck," Hon said to himself, and then he crossed the street.

"Juli—" He never completed her name. A cable broke and a half-dozen concrete columns fell from the twentieth floor. They smashed into the work site on the ground floor, through the wrought iron fence and onto the sidewalk.

Two of them landed directly on Hon.

Hearing the crash, Juliette turned. "Hon!" she screamed.

Nong, the security guard, ran to where Hon lay. He hung his head and sobbed. There was nothing he could do.

Hon was dead.

9

After Juliette's departure, the group had slowly slipped back into an air of Christmas cheer. A few bottles of Piper-Heidsieck Cuvée had been opened. Martin raised his glass and saluted, "*Chok dee.*" Everyone joined in the traditional Thai call for good luck.

"I truly wish you all a very Merry Christmas, my dear friends."

The glasses were drained and refilled and the party carried on as if there had been no rude interruption. After a few minutes, Tan got up and came to sit beside Martin in the empty chair recently vacated by Hon.

"Khun Martin, I feel I should go and check on Hon."

Martin smiled and put a hand on Tan's shoulder. "Hon always refers to you as *pee chai*, his older brother. But I think that neither his brother, or for that matter, his father, can help him with what he's dealing with right now."

"What is wrong with her?"

"I'm not sure. She can be quite charming. And then suddenly she morphs into what you saw tonight. Though I must admit, I've never seen her quite that over the top."

The front door opened and suddenly Virit was in the room with them.

"Virit. What is it?"

Virit put his hands together and bowed. "Khun Martin, please come with me."

"What are you talking about? We are having a party."

Virit spoke quietly into Soon's ear. She turned white and grabbed Areeya. "You must go with him. Now!"

Martin took Areeya's hand and headed for the door. The others started to follow but Virit held up his hand. "No. Please, just the master and the lady."

The ride in the elevator seemed an eternity to Martin. Areeya was squeezing his hand and hyperventilating. Virit remained stone-faced and quiet.

Downstairs, Martin and Areeya followed Virit down the jasmine-scented walk to Soi Langsuan.

By now there was a police motorcycle with a revolving light casting an eerie glow over the scene.

Martin inhaled deeply as Areeya gripped his arm with both hands. "Oh my God."

He and Areeya crossed the street without any caution. Virit held up his hand and stopped a line of taxis from running them down.

Without actually knowing, Martin feared what awaited them.

There were now a half-dozen construction workers and several police surrounding the horrific tableau. Six concrete columns, three meters in length with their internal rebar protruding, had fallen twelve floors to the pavement of Soi Langsuan. At least one had pierced Hon's skull, killing him instantly. The others had fallen onto the ground floor of the construction site. Judging by the sobbing, wailing, and mass confusion coming from the now crowded site, Hon was not the only victim.

Areeya fell to her knees, reaching for her son. Her hands

became red with his blood as she touched his chin and his lips. She began howling with sorrow and rage. Martin, his eyes overflowing with tears, attempted to console her. But she would not be consoled. She pummeled the lifeless body—willing it to rise and shake the unspeakable gore from its once handsome face.

There was nothing Martin could say or do to comfort her.

"Sir."

It took several long moments for Martin to remember where he was.

A young police officer was standing behind him. He had a notepad in his hand. "Sir…Can I have your name, please."

"What?"

"Your name. And your relationship to the…deceased."

A whistle was blown and an ambulance, its lights flashing red and blue, pulled to the curb. Several more were trying to get through the blocked traffic.

"Sir…Please, your name."

"Mar-Martin Larue."

"Is this your son?"

"What? Yes…Yes. He's our son."

The paramedics came with their gurney. Areeya gasped in horror when she saw them.

"No!" she screamed. "Don't touch him!" She gripped his arms and pulled his lifeless corpse to her.

She was now covered in blood. Martin, slightly less hysterical, attempted to get her to let go. But she would not.

"Please. Let him go. They must take him."

"No. He is *my* son…*Our* son. We will take him…*Upstairs*. He needs to be bathed…He needs…He needs…"

Nong and Virit gently put their hands on Areeya's shoulders, and she released her grip slightly. The paramedics, seeing the opportunity, stepped in and maneuvered the gurney into position.

Areeya finally let go and collapsed into Martin's arms, as the paramedics moved the body onto the gurney.

"Sir…His name, please."

Martin came out of his coma and realized the policeman was still standing alongside him.

Martin motioned to Nong, and he came and stood next the policeman. "This is Khun Nong. He is in charge of security for the building we live in just over there." He pointed and the officer noted the illuminated address. "He will give you whatever information you require at this point."

Martin turned to Nong. "Take this officer upstairs to the apartment. He may wish to interview the guests. Let him tell them there has been an accident. And have Khun Ben call me. We are going to the hospital."

Martin next addressed Virit, who, with the help of two other police, now had Areeya on her feet. "Virit, help us get into the ambulance and then wake up On and have him go to the hospital." He turned to the paramedics. "BNH?" They nodded. "Bangkok Nursing Home. Have him wait for us."

Martin turned to the police officer. "We are going to the hospital with our son. Khun Nong will give you all the help he can. There is a dinner party in progress in our apartment, and he will take you there. At the party is my attorney, Ben Waller. Introduce yourself and please allow him—and only him—to come down here. The others, after you question them, should be told to please return home with our apologies."

"Yes, sir." He handed Martin a business card. "We will be in touch. And sir?"

"Yes?"

"I am very sorry for your loss."

Ramonne admired the city from his rare perspective thirty floors above it on one of the newest architectural "gems"—the Park Hyatt Hotel. Its 24 floors of five-star luxury sat atop the Central Embassy mall. Ramonne was perched on the twisted spire that gave it a very unique outline. To his right—on the other side of the Chidlom skytrain platform, was another unique and beautiful skyscraper—the Okura Prestige Hotel.

He jumped off, and when he landed, the Okura was on his left. He thought to himself, *This flying off buildings like a bat—it never gets old.*

He descended in this manner to the roof of the skytrain platform. He had decided to hitch a ride on the top of one of the cars, and jump off near Soi 31 and his new home. But as soon as he landed on top of the station, it hit him. *Martin is near. He needs me.* He could feel Martin's presence. He could feel his pain. His sorrow, his overwhelming agony.

He leaped across to the Okura, ascended to the top, and then leapt into space with a hundred-foot construction crane as his target.

He dropped down the crane to the unfinished floor that it was using as its base. He surveyed the scene below. There was a small crowd, growing larger by the minute. An ambulance and emergency personnel had arrived.

He saw Martin. He saw Areeya. And he saw their adopted son, Hon. His lifeless body was being lifted onto a gurney.

Ramonne was frozen. He didn't move for three or four minutes.

And then slowly he descended. No one was watching the building. All eyes were on the tragedy. He stopped two floors above the scene.

He studied it. Patiently. Quietly.

Martin and Areeya rode in silence in the back of the ambulance. Martin had shed so many tears that his eyes and throat were dry. Areeya was the same.

The flashing lights and the siren caused some people to

move out of its way, but others, stubborn motorists, refused to move.

It made no difference. There no longer was an emergency. For all intents and purposes it was a coroner's van and not an ambulance.

The sheet had been pulled over Hon's body, but his hands were exposed. Areeya held on to his right one, and Martin held onto her.

"Turn them off please," Martin requested of the paramedics.

"Sir?"

"The lights…The siren. Please turn them off."

"We will not be able to jump the lanes. It will slow us down, sir."

"There is no rush. We all know that. Please let us ride in silence."

"As you wish, sir."

The siren and the lights were turned off. They now moved through the streets like a cold white shark.

————

Ramonne started to turn from the scene below and make his ascent, when he noticed a young woman watching the scene from the shadows of a car park entrance across the street.

A sense of darkness and fear emanated from her—but also a sense of connection to the tragedy—and Ramonne decided that he should follow her.

At least until the coming of the dawn.

10

The Bangkok Nursing Home was founded in 1898 under the patronage of King Rama V. It was the first private hospital in Thailand, and its colonial construction and abnormally solid and secure basement attracted Ramonne Delacroix who, at that time, had been a nighttime denizen of Bangkok for a little over thirty years. He bribed a contractor to build a secret series of rooms and an entrance in the sub-basement, and then proceeded to eliminate anyone who knew of the subterfuge.

The vampire lived there for another thirty years, leaving only when it was remodeled in the early 1950s.

Modern Bangkok has many world-class hospitals and has become well-known as a center for medical tourism. Have your face-lift or gall bladder operation in Bangkok, and recover while lying under a coconut palm in one of the luxury resorts in the south. At a fraction of what the operation alone would cost elsewhere.

Martin preferred this particular hospital over the others, for it seemed less ostentatious and more personal. And he had a physician, Dr. Irene—last name unpronounceable and unspellable—who had been his personal doctor for going on 25 years. She was known in the expat community as "House" after the popular physician-cum-detective played by Hugh Laurie on TV.

Nina was born here. A deadly game of cat-and-mouse was played here when the Japanese Black Dragons kidnapped his wife, and he and Ramonne were forced to track them to the Hernando Cemetery, and Ramonne sacrificed himself to save the mother and unborn child.

But tonight the hospital was merely a depository. A storage facility for the remains of Martin and Areeya's beloved son.

The sterility of the white walls somehow made Areeya cringe.

She was being scrubbed by a nurse who was already sterile, but in helping Areeya out of her blood-soaked clothing, she too was getting contaminated with Hon's precious blood.

Areeya watched it roll down the drain…Her son's *life*.

In another room, Martin was also being cleaned up. He sat on a stool as a nurse removed his shirt and wiped his face and hands with disinfectant.

He stared blankly forward, waiting for the process to finish.

She handed him a white smock, which he pulled over his head. She put his shirt in a plastic bag and told him it would be given to his driver.

He stepped into the hall, looking oddly like a surgeon ready for "prep." In a few moments, Areeya appeared, looking less surgical and more like a nun. He pulled her to him and they had another quiet cry on each other's sanitary shoulders.

"Sir."

Without looking, Martin knew who it was. He stopped a passing nurse and asked her to find Areeya an empty bed.

Then he turned to the young policeman. "Yes?"

"I don't mean to bother you in your time of mourning. But I must ask a few questions."

"I have a question myself. What is your name?"

"Sergeant Prasert Theeravit, sir." He clicked his heels and saluted.

"Sir, I have talked to the guests at your party and they say there was an argument between your son and the young lady who accompanied him."

"Actually she argued not only with my son, but with my wife and several others. She was drunk."

"And then she and your son left the party?"

"Yes. And that's all I know. They were gone for twenty minutes or so when Khun Virit, the doorman, came up and asked us to follow him downstairs. From that point, I believe you were there."

"Yes. I arrived the same time you did."

The same nurse that had escorted Areeya was waiting patiently in the hall.

"You must excuse me, Sergeant Prasert, but I need to go and see to my wife."

"Of course."

The nurse started to escort Martin when he stopped and turned back to the policeman.

"Sergeant Prasert, I have another question. Why is your English so good?"

"I studied abroad, sir."

"Where?"

"Cambridge."

Martin was surprised. "Cambridge?"

"Yes, sir. I got a scholarship."

'You studied at Cambridge but you returned to Bangkok to become a policeman?"

"Yes, sir. I feel my country needs educated police."

"Well, that certainly is true...And, frankly, quite noble."

The nurse took Martin to Areeya's room.

She was sitting on the edge of the bed, her head in her hands. He sat next to her, put his arm around her, and she looked up.

"What do we do now?"

"I don't know…Sign some papers. Go home. Arrange a funeral. I really don't know."

"I don't want a funeral. I want my son."

"I know you do."

"Khun Martin?"

It was an administrator for the hospital. You could tell by the formal dress, even at 2:00 a.m.

"Yes?"

"Would you please sign these release documents. They permit the hospital to take care of your son's remains while you make arrangements."

Martin sighed. "Everything is so…*final*."

He signed the papers.

"Thank you. And I'm so sorry for your loss."

He nodded.

There was a "ping" and the elevator opened.

Ben emerged from it, looking rumpled and worn. Martin saw him and they embraced. "Martin, I'm so sorry."

Martin said nothing, just accepted the solid male embrace of a friend.

Finally Martin spoke. "What happened after we left?"

"We had no idea what was going on until that young policeman showed up. He asked each of us, starting with me, what had happened in the hour or so after Hon and Juliette arrived and left."

Martin made a conscious effort to clear his head for the first time since the horror happened. "Do the guests know what happened?"

"No. They do not. They were told there was an emergency and that they should go home. He said you asked that only I should go downstairs with him, which I did."

"And Krystal?"

"She went with Tan and Katy."

"What time was this?"

"Approximately ten o'clock. You were gone. The ambulances were gone. There was blood and gore and shattered concrete pillars—which were hurriedly scooped up by the construction workers. The battered chain-link fence was reinstalled and a heavy black cloth was hung around the fence—obliterating any view of the site."

"It was a *crime scene!*"

"It *was*. But it was quickly obliterated."

"How is that possible?"

"Martin, how long have you lived here…thirty years?"

Martin nodded. "Then you shouldn't be asking me that question. The police took photos and so did I."

Martin clearly could not process any more. His brain was about to shut down. "Ben, I *need* you."

"And you *have* me. I'm with you on this. We will bring your son's *murderers*—because that's who I believe they are, murderers—to justice. But it won't be easy."

Martin suddenly felt very alone as he looked around the huge hospital corridors where everyday life and death played out in an endless arena, and realized he was now just a bit player.

"Go home, Martin. Your son is here. Next you will put him to rest. *Our* fight will start after that."

Martin hugged Ben and then helped his wife to her shaky feet and, with Virit's help, made it outside to the BMW.

———

Christmas…It's Christmas Day.

This thought struck Martin as he sank into his chair and stared out the window at the false dawn that preceded the winter sunrise in Bangkok by about an hour.

A doctor had checked both he and Areeya before they left the hospital, and prescribed sleeping tablets for each of them. Areeya took hers and was finally resting in her own bed.

Martin didn't want anything to interfere with his thoughts

until he couldn't stand it anymore—and then he would seek sleep. But now he sat in the dark apartment and studied the decorations that had seemed so warm and inviting just hours earlier, and now seemed cold and callous.

Soon had silently admitted them when they arrived. There was nothing to say, and so they simply went and checked on Nina while Soon went to bed.

Nina was sleeping the sleep of the innocent, and apart from Areeya's kiss on her forehead, they let her slumber undisturbed.

She'll awake soon. Of course she will. She's a little girl. And it's Christmas. Martin wasn't sure how he would deal with that. Nina was a *luk khreung*, meaning her parents were of Thai and foreign origin. Therefore, though they didn't celebrate all of the Thai holidays, the major western holidays that Martin grew up with were traditions in the Larue household. Thanksgiving, Christmas Eve and Christmas Day, New Year's Eve and New Year's Day.

Martin, having been born Protestant and never deeply religious, had taken to the simple aspects of Theravada Buddhism that his Thai wife practiced. He had spent an entire year as a monk after the shock and horror of his initial encounter with the vampire Ramonne. But subsequently he became more relaxed in his acceptance of any and all religions.

Hon had basically been an atheist, causing many arguments with his mother, which Martin preferred to stay out of.

What do I say to her?

Perhaps, he thought, *its best to say nothing to Nina for a while. Why spoil the joy of Christmas morning for her?*

He remembered that Santa's gifts for her were in his office. He reluctantly rose from the chair and went to retrieve them.

———

The boy. Gone. Forever.

And there was nothing he could do about it.

Ramonne sat in his study and sipped his wine—staring at nothing. He remembered the first time he had encountered the mind of a child.

He had been sent by Ping to Paris to take out an old enemy. But Ping didn't want the enemy killed—he wanted his son dead. In revenge for an event in the past that cost Ping his oldest son.

But the man's son was merely a child. When Ramonne approached him, he was sleeping. Ramonne was overwhelmed. The aura the child projected was so pure and innocent that he could hardly breathe.

Ramonne controlled adults by crawling into the crevices of their minds and manipulating their deepest fears. But with the boy, there was no fear. No trepidation. No hesitation. The boy was dreaming. Anything was possible to the boy. His vision of life was...*magical*.

Ramonne did not kill the boy. He *could not*.

He had nothing to do with children for many years after that. He was in awe of them and yet he had an inane *fear* of them. Until Martin established the orphanage in Siem Reap and Ramonne was forced to do battle with the thousand-year-old vampire Zhoupeng. He enlisted Martin and the child he considered his "son"—five-year-old Hon. In the ensuing battle, Hon "died." He lay motionless, not breathing, while Martin ranted and raved and cursed the vampire. But the vampire told Martin that the boy was not dead, and when he laid his hand on his forehead, the boy's eyes opened.

In later days, the boy actually referred to Ramonne once, to Martin's intense agitation, as "Daddy." Martin had, as yet, not heard those words from the boy, and was infuriatingly jealous.

It had a significant impact on Martin's decision to move the family from Siem Reap back to Bangkok.

Ramonne smiled as he thought of the boy. He was incredibly sad that he didn't know the man the boy had become. He had deliberately stayed away from Martin since his return. But this tragedy was not going to be easy to erase from anyone's mind.

He felt Martin's pain, and vowed to do anything he could to ease his suffering.

Before he shut the door of the vault, he thought about the girl he had followed. She was scared. Extremely so. Her mind was delirious—clouded by chemicals. He could sense the deep connection to the boy. But there was a dark cloud over her. There was little for him to read in the jumble of emotions that were tumbling forth as she moved through the city. Eventually she caught a cab and he followed her to the port at Khlong Toey. There she entered a decrepit hotel.

Ramonne left, knowing he could pick up her trail there if he needed to.

———

Santa Claus's workshop for this year was behind Martin's desk in his office.

There was a large but fairly flat box, which held a Magic Princess Castle Tent. Martin dragged it out into the hall and slid it to the living room.

Slicing it open with a small Swiss Army knife that he always had in his pocket—except, unfortunately, on airplanes—he pulled out the sections of diaphanous material that would give the castle its glow when the fairy lights were hung inside and lit.

The directions, not complicated, were in Thai. Not a problem for Martin. He was completely fluent, reading and writing, in Thai, Chinese—Mandarin and Cantonese—and Japanese.

No tools were required, and within half an hour the Magic Princess Castle Tent was fully assembled and glowing alongside the Christmas tree.

Martin realized this exercise had been very therapeutic. He hadn't actually thought of Hon for thirty or forty minutes. He picked up the remnants of the box and the packing, and took them back to his office.

There was another, much smaller, present also stored behind his desk. This one he opened in the office. It was a Kidizoom Duo digital camera, designed as a first camera for children, with lots of child-friendly features including an automatic shut-off after three minutes of inactivity.

He carried it into the living room and set it down inside the Princess tent. He sat back down in his chair and, just before he could slip into his depression again, there she was.

Rubbing sleepy eyes, clothed in pink pajamas that encased her toes like socks, little Nina slowly came awake.

Martin remained silent. He was certain he was invisible to her. Her gaze was laser-fixed on the Magic Princess Castle Tent.

Those beautiful dark eyes of the soon-to-be eight-year-old girl widened.

Her smile filled the entire room—overwhelming the rosy dawn creeping through the windows. She scurried across the floor and fell at the foot of the fairytale tent. Within seconds she was inside.

Martin had not moved since she appeared.

Suddenly there was a howl of joy from inside the tent. Martin knew she had discovered the camera.

Quietly Martin got out of his chair walked down the hall.

———

Ben's law office was in the Capital Tower at All Seasons Place. His clients were mainly Americans and other English-speaking expats. The convenient access to both the American and British embassies was appreciated by the lawyers and their clients.

He was seated at his desk when Martin appeared. He stood and shook Martin's hand.

"Thank you, Ben, for coming in today to see me."

"Not a problem. We usually don't close during Christmas

and New Year. Our staff and most of the lawyers just take shorter hours. The Thai courts are open this week and we all take a week off in April for the Thai new year."

"Good. Now I don't feel so bad.

"Sit, please."

Martin sat down in a very comfortable chair that somehow placed him slightly lower than Ben sitting behind his desk. Ben had a file folder open before him.

"I also want to thank you for keeping Hon's name out of the press…so far."

Ben looked Martin in the eye before he replied. "That won't last much longer. Hon wasn't the only victim. There were three workers killed and two seriously wounded."

Martin was stunned. "My God. Six victims. Four deaths. Those poor people. Were they at the hospital with us?"

"No. They were at Chulalongkorn Hospital."

This was a public hospital run by the national health system. Martin had ended up in the hospital's emergency room once— not very pleasant—but they turned no one away.

"I don't mean to be crude, but how does this affect our case?"

"I don't know yet. Two of the dead workers and one of the wounded are Burmese. It's not known yet whether they were registered to work or not. This is a regular problem with construction in Thailand. I suspect they were *not* registered. It may delay getting our case onto the court docket."

Ben closed the folder and leaned back in his chair waiting for Martin's reply.

"I want to get a start on this. I know you said 'Bury your son, and then we'll get the bastards.' But I can't wait that long."

"Martin. What exactly are the funeral arrangements?"

"The body has been in the temple for two days. Each evening our family and friends and Hon's friends gather to watch a dozen monks do endless chants."

"I'm sorry we haven't been there. Krystal has a very hard time with funerals. I will come to the cremation."

"Thank you. Frankly it's all starting to drive me nuts—that's why I came here. I need to start to do something about what happened."

"Martin, let me tell you something about Thai law."

"By all means, educate me."

"First of all, I'm your attorney, but I cannot plead your case in a Thai court. I'm a foreigner. But, we have excellent Thai litigators."

"Ben, I don't care if it's you or your Thai appointee. I care about what we are doing."

"We will file a negligence charge against the building owner and contractors. We will also file a separate criminal lawsuit. But do not expect any of this to be swift."

"Who are we dealing with?"

"That's complicated. We've only just started to investigate."

Martin leaned back and crossed his arms. "Speculate."

"Lawyers don't do that. It's not fair to their clients."

"Ben, you're not telling me something."

"No. I'm telling you everything I know. So far."

"Ben. Someone took my son from me. That someone must be made to pay."

"Martin. That is my mission—but be prepared for a long fight."

———

Satisfied, bloodlust fulfilled, Ramonne dropped the body unceremoniously into the Chao Phraya River.

He'd seen the supposed sea captain ply his trade on the waterfront for weeks now. He'd approach down-on-their-luck Thais in the Khlong Toey slums. Young men with families to feed. The pitch was always the same: "Go to sea under contract.

Return thirty days later with a fat wallet and the start of a new life."

Except what happened was that the young men were "shanghaied"—a term Ramonne first heard in 1859 when he accompanied the French explorer Henri Mahout on his second expedition to the mysterious east. Ships needed crews, but working conditions were bad, so crews were often obtained by trickery, bribery, force, and outright kidnapping. Sometimes a man would be offered drinks until he passed out, then would awaken on board and under way. In the current case, the sailor would be forced to work twenty hours a day as a virtual slave on Thai fishing boats, and perhaps never see his family again.

Over the past century, Ramonne had found the port of Khlong Toey to be a veritable treasure trove of homeless, nameless souls for his weekly forays in search of sustenance. He had long ago established that he only needed to feed on human blood but once or twice a week; anything else was gluttony.

But having discovered that the "Shanghai trade" was still in practice allowed him to focus on its perpetrators as his new favored targets.

Sated, he was about to head to the rooftops, when he saw *her*.

The girl from the accident scene. The one he followed that night to the seedy hotel not far from where he was now.

He hadn't actually thought of her since then. He thought of Martin, of course. He knew that soon he would encounter Martin, but first he needed to let him grieve.

But here was the girl. Somehow, she was a part of what had happened.

She was wearing the same dress she wore that night. Now it was wrinkled and worn and her hair was in disarray.

There was a man with her. An *evil* man, Ramonne surmised, without a touch of irony. He crept closer and soon what was transpiring was clear to him. The man had just had sex with the girl. Not intercourse, but the girl had performed sex *on* him.

In the shadow of a doorway he handed her something.

Drugs. No doubt. Payment for services rendered.

The man departed and the girl turned back towards the hotel. Ramonne followed her briefly, attempting to unlock the mystery of why she would have anything to do with the death of Martin's son. Or anything to do with Martin's world at all? But he couldn't penetrate the dark wall that enshrouded her mind. He attributed it to her drug addiction.

He decided to leave her for now and visit an old friend.

———

"Martin, darling. We have to go"

Martin sat in the kitchen with a bottle of Grey Goose vodka and a tumbler of ice.

"Why?"

"Because it's what we do…it's how we honor our son's memory."

"I can't. Really. I can't. I can't spend another hour thanking people for their concern, their sympathy, their pity. I can't do it anymore."

Areeya bent down and hugged him. "I know, darling. But they will be there. All of them."

"Really. I can't do it again. Tell them I'm sick. Lord knows I am. They'll believe you."

Areeya sighed. "All right, my darling. Are you sure you'll be okay?"

"Yes. What I need is to be alone. That would be the best thing in the world for me right now."

Areeya kissed him and held him for a long moment and then she took little Nina's hand, who had been waiting patiently by the door, and they left.

Martin sat in the kitchen with the opened bottle and the ice for a long time before rising and taking them both with him.

It had taken less than 24 hours to get the body moved from

the hospital to the temple Areeya wanted. There was a bathing ceremony the next day, attended by Areeya and her mother. They washed the body, and dressed it. Normally the hair would have been shampooed but due to the disfigurement, a wax skin had been placed over the wound on the skull, giving Hon the appearance of having a shaved skull. The coffin was closed for the funeral ceremonies that started that evening and went on for six evenings. All friends and family were invited, and a dozen Buddhist monks chanted in unison each evening for an hour. Afterwards there was a light meal and much emotion.

The final funeral ceremony would be the next evening, New Year's Eve, Nina's birthday, and the cremation was on New Year's Day.

Martin sat in the enclosed porch that faced Lumpini Park. The Christmas tree in the living room behind him had been taken down. No one could face it anymore. He finally poured the thick vodka over the tumbler of ice. He took a long sip and relished the feeling as the vodka warmed his inner being.

The evening lights of the park and the surrounding skyscrapers sparkled against the jet-black sky. Thailand was at its most temperate at this time of year, and the wooden shutters and the double-glazed windows were open and an inviting breeze wafted into the room.

Martin took another deep drink and he realized he was not alone.

Most men would have panicked. Or cried out. But for Martin this was a familiar occurrence. He merely smiled.

"Don't you ever knock."

"Now what would be the fun in that?" Ramonne replied. He was seated in the darkest corner of the room.

"Welcome back."

"Thank you."

Martin realized he was toasting with his glass. "Sorry...Wine?"

"Of course."

Martin went to a small wine cooler and opened it. He selected a bottle of Clos Pegase Pinot Noir. A nice little red wine with a twist top—which was actually the reason he chose it. He handed the glass to Ramonne.

"Thank you."

They drank in silence for several minutes.

Finally Martin spoke. "Last time I saw you—nine years ago —you were being consumed by hellfire. Should I ask how you manage to be here now?"

"Probably best not to. I'm not completely sure myself."

"All right…Then why are you here?

"Aren't you glad to see me?"

"Yes, of course, but your appearance after so many years is…*shocking*."

"And yet, somehow I get the feeling you were expecting me."

"I heard about Phuket."

"Ahh. Yes. That was interesting."

"So, it was you."

"Yes."

More silence.

Then: "I'm here to help you, Martin. I know where the girl is."

"What girl?"

"The girl. The one who left the scene."

"What scene?"

"The scene of the accident. That killed your son."

"You were there?"

"No. Not when it happened—but shortly after. I saw you getting into an ambulance and I saw the girl in the shadows, hiding. So I followed her."

"You followed her?"

"Yes. I thought she might have been involved."

"And what did you find out?"

"Nothing. She's a drug addict. Her mind is blank to me."

Martin stared at Ramonne, and then he put his glass down on the table very gently. "Do you know who she is…? She was my son's girlfriend. She caused him to wander out into the street on Christmas Eve, where a construction crane let slip a half-dozen concrete beams—instantly crushing his skull. But to you she's *blank*? You know nothing about her?"

Martin was sweating. He gulped the glass of vodka and poured another, which he also started to down.

Ramonne put his hand on the glass.

"I didn't know any of that, Martin. Calm down. Mortals don't deal well with death. Take deep breaths."

"I'll take deep breaths…when you bring her to me. She caused my son's death as much as that contractor did."

Martin collapsed back in his chair and quietly wept.

Ramonne studied Martin silently. His pain and grief were overwhelming. The montage of images that he picked up on in just a few moments were staggering. The young innocent boy. The child prodigy and the proud parents. And then the horror of the discovery of his body in the street. Interspersed were brief glimpses of the girl. Her arrival in Bangkok, her obvious influence on the boy, and some sort of disturbance at the dinner just prior to his death.

Ramonne put his hand on Martin's shoulder. "I will bring her to you."

11

Hon's funeral was as formal as a dozen bare-footed, orange-robed monks could make it. Six 16 x 20 inch framed photos of him were displayed on easels, and the temple overflowed with flowers with sweet messages attached. There were too many wreaths to fit in the room, so several were displayed outside the entrance.

The closed casket stood in front of the chanting monks.

On this final evening, New Year's Eve, all Martin could think of was Norman Greenbaum's song "Spirit in the Sky" and a wish that it was being blasted right now through the temple speakers instead of the continual chanting. He knew the monks were performing the ceremony in the only manner they knew, and he appreciated the dignity they brought to his son's undignified demise. He just wished he could change the music.

He wasn't sure his son's friends appreciated it. He wasn't sure *his* friends appreciated it. But he knew that his wife—a beautiful, good Thai woman—was laying to rest not just their son, but *her* son.

There would be no party. No New Orleans-style Second Line brass band parade. Nothing that irreverent.

Tonight they were chanting for their son on his way to nirvāna.

———

"Martin, darling, are you okay?"

They were in bed. The final funeral ceremony had gone on to 10 p.m., New Year's Eve. While most of the guests went off to a party somewhere, Martin, Nina, and Areeya went home.

"Yes…You?"

She snuggled into his arms. "I suppose. It's all so bizarre."

"I know."

"Did you say 'happy birthday' to Nina?"

"Yes. And I told her we would celebrate next week. She said, 'That's okay. We don't have to.' I couldn't believe it. She's stronger than I am."

"She did the same with me. I couldn't bear it."

"How is that possible?"

"She's a kid. They're innocent. That makes them strong."

"Let's try and keep her innocent."

They lay quietly. A dozen candles flickered gently. Martin's thoughts drifted to Ramonne, and he knew he had to tell her.

He sat up.

"He's back."

Areeya sat up and pushed him away.

"What do you mean? He's *here*?"

"Bangkok. Our home…Last night."

"Martin. I really don't know what to say."

"Say nothing. Let me deal with him. Remember, he saved your life. And Nina's."

"I know that. But he's a fucking *vampire*, Martin."

"I also know that. Very well. But he is no threat to us. And he could actually help us."

"*Help* us?"

"Yes. There are powerful people involved in the accident

that killed our son. Ben says we have to be very careful. With Ramonne helping us, maybe we don't have to be *as* careful. Maybe we can get some justice."

"*Justice*? Is that what you want?"

"Yes."

Areeya turned her back on him and pulled a nightgown over her shoulders. "All I want now is to scatter Hon's ashes. Honor his memory…Justice can wait."

Martin looked at her and she lay back down on the bed.

Outside, fireworks began exploding over Lumpini Park to welcome in the new year.

Martin got up and closed the blinds and curtains without glancing at the pyrotechnics.

He blew out the candles, climbed back in the bed, and pulled Areeya to him.

———

January

The next day was the worst day of Martin's life. It rivaled the day when he knew Hon was gone. But this was the day when they would dispose of his body forever.

Cremate him.

Until now there was a body. It lay in a box in front of them for a week. "Don't miracles happen? Didn't Jesus rise from the dead? Didn't Ramonne return again and again? So why not my son? My beautiful, talented, sweet son?"

The ceremony was mercifully short. Then the boy was borne by his peers, friends, and his father. They all hoisted the casket up the steep stairs of the crematorium.

Packed daily with fresh ice, the coffin and the boy were extremely heavy. All were sweating when their labor was done.

The coffin was rolled onto a chute that would slowly channel it into the crematorium. As the coffin-bearers made their way back down the stairs, it began its slow journey…into the fire.

Martin and the others returned to their loved ones. Their hands were cleaned by caring monks who knew that the ice around the body had leaked out onto the coffin-bearers' hands.

Solemnly they waited outside the crematorium and watched the smoke slowly rise through the chimney. The smoke was gray as the ceremony began, but within ten minutes it turned white—a sign that the body was being consumed by fire.

People stayed for an hour or so after the cremation, giving their condolences to Martin and Areeya and each other. Then slowly they drifted away.

———

Martin opened the envelope. Inside was a single sheet containing a few typed notes.

"This is it?"

"That's all I could find. She's a ghost. No trail."

"Fuck." Martin crumpled the paper into a ball.

"You can burn that if you like. But I sent it to your email. When you want to know who she is, start by actually reading it…She is not a student at Parsons in Paris. That's pretty much who she is *not*. It seems she may actually be from Provence. There is a birth certificate registered for a Juliette Dorval at the Hotel de Ville in La Coste. The '*Hotel de Ville*' is the 'city hall' in France."

"I know. Go on."

"However, that woman was born in 1776. There are no records of any siblings or children who might have passed on the name. But I assume that woman was her sixth great-grandmother."

"That's the name she uses."

"Future generations often take on the name of a favored relative. That would not be recorded in La Coste if she were born in another province. And, unfortunately, France's public records are not as current as they could be.

Colin McGavin shifted a little in his comfortable chair. They were at the Oriental Hotel in the Author's Lounge. Martin knew it would be empty on the afternoon of New Year's Day.

Martin sighed. "This is all you have?"

"Yes. That's it. She's a ghost."

Martin poured them each another glass of the Venetian Prosecco he had ordered.

"Thank you my friend. You did what you could."

"Martin. Let me say—"

Martin put up a hand. "Stop, Colin…I know how you feel. You don't have to say anything."

———

Martin stayed in the Author's Lounge after Colin departed. The white-on-white two-story tearoom was a garden pond until the mid-1970s. It was here that Ramonne took Martin on his first mind-bending journeys back in time. Subsequent tales from Ramonne regarding his experiences after World War II gave Martin insight into the history of the hotel.

The salon's walls were covered in history. Black-and-white photos chronicled Bangkok growing through the years. When Ramonne took Martin on his first foray through these hallowed halls and the photos came to life, Martin thought he was losing his mind.

He probably was. And he probably did.

But he had no regrets…not involving his association with Ramonne. However, his thoughts currently were not on Ramonne, in spite of the shock of his return. There was nothing on Martin's mind other than thoughts of his beloved son.

He remembered something the guitar player John told him on the first night of the funeral. He was waiting patiently to talk with Martin, who was besieged by friends and relatives giving their condolences.

Finally they were alone together. Fortunately, John did not plunge into the usual genuflecting, but instead he told Martin that he felt Hon had some premonition of his death.

"The album we were going to record—it was titled *Yang Yu*. Hon said that was Thai for—"

Martin interrupted him, "Still here."

"Yes. Sorry, Mr. Larue."

"Martin…please."

"Martin…I think he had a feeling *something* was coming. There was a song on the album titled 'I Am Home.' He had conversations with us about death—saying things like 'I am always' and 'Death is only of the body.' He was younger than me…just eighteen. Why was he thinking of death?"

"I have no idea."

Actually, Martin had a *few* ideas. Subconsciously, Hon could have been affected by all the childhood trauma he had been subjected to. It would certainly have been enough to send many others to psychiatrist couches for years, but not Hon. He appeared to have been completely unaffected by it. Or so it seemed.

But the more Martin thought about it, he realized Hon was withdrawn and closed off until he discovered the piano.

The last thing that John said to Martin touched him deeply.

"We want to finish the record. Simon says we can use Hon's rehearsal tracks. They're perfect. All we need to do is bring our own tracks up to his level…We wanted you to know."

"Thank you. I think that's wonderful."

———

"Okay. Here's what's happening."

Martin was back in Ben's office. Ben had a file in front of him, and took a slim folder and opened it.

"The court filing was made. The defendants responded with a rebuttal. They were polite—but firm."

"That means they're saying they're not responsible?"

"They're saying they followed all safety procedures, but that the fault of the accident lay with the operator of the crane, the men who loaded the crane, and in the crane itself."

"In other words, they don't want us to sue them."

"We're nowhere near that point, Martin. They're saying they're not guilty. This is the first phase. They will put up a crane operator and a couple of Burmese workers who loaded the concrete pilings. They'll offer them up to the police—sacrificial lambs, as it were."

"And what happens to them?"

"They get arrested." He consulted a file. "In fact...they've already been arrested."

"And what are they charged with?"

"Manslaughter...Normally five to fifteen years imprisonment. However there has been a request filed with the court to increase the penalty to life—hoping that imprisoning them for the rest of their miserable lives will make you happy and go away."

"That's absurd."

"I know."

"I want to hold someone responsible for what happened to my son."

"So do I. But it will be a landmark case. Tradition dictates that it is much more convenient to blame a lesser individual, always an unnamed official, whose punishment will remain hidden behind a veil of secrecy."

He opened another file and pulled out a sheet of paper. "The developer. That is who we want to target. They released this statement to the press, the day of the cremation: 'On behalf—'"

"What's his name?"

"Vithiya Sarawat."

"I want to meet with him"

"He won't meet with you."

"He came to the cremation ceremony."

Ben puts down his papers.

"There was a commotion. A fleet of black Mercedes arrived and a man approached Areeya. She became very upset and asked him to please leave."

"No. That wasn't him. That was one of his lawyers."

"Who is he?"

"Let's just say he's someone you don't want to *mess* with."

"I don't want to mess with him. I want him to admit that his construction site was not safe, and that was the reason for my son's death."

Ben sighed. "Again...so do I. But we have to take this slowly. And cautiously."

"Not my style, Ben."

"I know...unfortunately."

12

February

"Master. You are sure the woman is still in residence?"

Ramonne looked sideways at Professor Kaestle. He was in the passenger seat of a white Nissan van, recently stolen from a Central department store parking lot. It was just like thousands of others in the city, and passed anonymously through the crowded streets.

"Yes. I'm sure. And I'm sure she will leave that decrepit *residence* in less than twenty minutes, as she does most nights. Seeking her *connection*, I believe they call it. For her fix."

"Very good, sir. Just checking."

Ramonne stared at the professor again, and then went back to watching the door to the hotel. They were on a stakeout, as he informed the professor last night. The van had to be procured because they needed to transport the girl back to Martin's without harm. Dragging her across rooftops and up the side of skyscrapers might not ensure that outcome.

Suddenly there she was.

She had a light shawl draped over her shoulders, and she

seemed to have lost even more weight than when he last saw her two days ago.

Ramonne nodded to the professor and got out of the van. He moved slowly through the shadows towards the girl, pausing midway between her and the van.

Behind him, the professor also got out, and opened the side door. He then got back behind the wheel.

When the girl was within reach, Ramonne stepped out of the shadows and approached her. He did not speak. But she stopped. And turned.

That was all it took. Ramonne's eyes met hers. She paused momentarily and made a hissing sound before capitulating. But she was under his spell. He merely pointed to the van.

He got in the back with her, and closed the door.

———

Martin was in his study. Trying to read. Ben had given him the latest court documents and their translations.

The apartment was empty. Areeya and Nina were at her mother's for the acceptance of the ashes. Soon, Hon would reside in an earthen jar on their mantle. Except they didn't have a mantle. And so it was decided that there would be a shrine erected in their apartment—to be moved whenever they moved —as well as another one in the orphanage in Siem Reap. The ashes were to be divided fifty percent to each.

But that didn't concern Martin at the moment. At the moment he just wanted to know. *What the fuck happened?*

Why had two thousand pounds of concrete come crashing down on his son's head on a public sidewalk? How could a construction project be so negligent as to swing crane loads over unprotected pedestrian traffic? Why were the loads on the crane unsecured?

And why was his son on the sidewalk in the first place?

He never should have been there. He should have been safe

in the confines of Martin's apartment sixteen floors above the accident on the opposite side of the street.

He collapsed back in his chair, mentally exhausted.

He had only a few precious moments of quiet peace before the doorbell chimed. He waited for Soon to answer it before he realized she was off duty this evening. He opened the door—completely unprepared for what greeted him.

"Professor Kaestle…To what do I owe this honor?

Sheepishly the professor stepped aside, revealing Ramonne and the girl in the elevator.

"Sorry, Martin, but I needed the professor to act as decoy with your doorman."

Martin crossed his arms. "Pray tell me, how does that work?"

Ramonne stepped out of the elevator with the somnambulant girl. "Really, Martin, let's not play games. You wanted her to come here. And now here she is."

They sat in the living room. Professor Kaestle brewed tea for Martin, and opened a bottle of wine for Ramonne. The girl sat on the couch, vacant-eyed.

Martin was anxious to begin. "All right. Let's get started."

"You must understand, this is the first time I've had any control over her. She came out of the hotel, as I suspected, fairly clean of drugs. She was in search of them. That's why I was able to control her and bring her to you. But I truly know nothing about her…she is unique to me."

"Fine. I just want to know what her relationship with my son truly was. So, please…release her."

Ramonne did nothing more than look at her. Intensely. Within a few moments she regained consciousness. She was awake, but not aware of her surroundings.

"Ask her who she is?"

"You can ask her, Martin. You no longer need me."

Without further prompting she answered, "Juliette Dorval."

"Do you know who I am?"

"Yes. Hon's father."

"Do you know where you are?"

"Yes. In your apartment."

"Do you remember the last time you were here?"

"Yes. It was Christmas Eve."

"There was a party. Do you remember that?"

"Yes."

"You and Hon left the party. Do you remember why?"

"Yes...we had a fight."

"Why did you fight?"

Silence.

"Juliette?"

Silence.

"All right. You had a fight and you wanted to leave."

"Yes. I hated the party."

"Why?"

"It was a bunch of bourgeois intellectuals and pompous assholes."

"Did you consider Hon a *pompous asshole*?"

"He was encouraging them."

"So you decided to leave?"

"*He* decided."

"You didn't want to leave?"

"I did."

"So you went down the elevator to the street. Did you fight in the elevator going down?"

"I suppose so...I don't remember."

"When you got off the elevator, what happened?"

"I told him to fuck off. And I started on the path to the street."

"I assume he followed."

"He did."

"And then?"

"I just wanted to get away from him."

"So what did you do?"

"I crossed the street."

"He followed you?"

"Yes."

"And then?"

She paused. "Then there was a tremendous sound and I turned back. He was crushed by all this concrete and there was blood everywhere."

"What did you do?"

"I shrank into the shadows and I watched."

"You watched?"

"Yes. I watched...I watched people run to his side. I watched traffic come to a stop, and I watched people get out of their cars and stare in shock and horror. I watched people come down from the construction site. I watched police arrive...I watched *you* arrive."

"You *watched*?"

"Yes. I watched. What else could I do?"

"And then what did you do?"

"I left."

"You left?"

"Yes. I left."

She had been vacant-eyed and turned away from Martin throughout the entire exchange. But now she turned back and faced him. Her eyes were dark and hollow.

"I left...What was I supposed to do?"

At that point Martin looked at Ramonne and nodded, and Ramonne put Juliette under again.

"What do you think?" Martin asked.

"There is *something*...I don't know yet what it is. When I approached her, she resisted."

"Yes?"

"Normally there is complete capitulation. It is much easier for a mortal to give their mind to someone else to control than to resist an unknown, powerful force. But she challenged me. She actually *hissed* at me." He shrugged. "And yet, she says what she feels. What she knows. What you would call the *truth*. Some would challenge that. I accept it…But I don't yet know who she really is."

"I don't know either. I asked someone to look into her, and he found nothing. Said she's a ghost. But she's the only witness to my son's death."

"Is that important?"

"It could be."

"So you need her?"

"Yes."

"I don't think she intends to stay in Bangkok long."

"Try to keep her here. But don't harm her."

Ramonne smiled. "A pleasure. I'd like to know her better."

Professor Kaestle took the girl down to the van, leaving Ramonne and Martin alone. They sat quietly for several long moments.

Finally Ramonne spoke. "You've been through the Buddhist funeral ceremonies for your son. I'm sorry."

"It was hell."

"You're an honest man. Most would say it was 'beautiful.' Something about how he can now rest his eternal soul. Etcetera, etcetera."

"It was worse than I ever imagined. It dragged on for an entire week. No one's fault. It is what it is. But it was extremely painful for me. A reminder that we have no control over our departure."

"Perhaps it's best to prolong that departure."

"Easy for you to say."

"I meant no offense. I just truly…at this age, can't imagine what it's like to be mortal."

Martin sighed. "You know what I want? What I really want?"

Ramonne waited.

"I want *revenge*."

"Revenge?"

"Yes. That's what I want."

"Against who?"

"Whoever's responsible."

"Who do you think that is?"

"For a while I thought it might be the girl."

"And now?"

"And now I know. It's the developer. He ran an unsafe construction site."

"Do you have a name?"

———

Martin and Ben emerged from the stuffy confines of the ancient courthouse into the haze that now seems a regular part of everyday life in today's Bangkok.

The session had lasted two hours, with Ben's Thai team attempting to introduce evidence of the negligence they had documented at the construction site. They were systematically challenged by the massive number of attorneys opposing them. Although the junior assistants came and went, Martin at one point counted fourteen on the opposing side. He and Ben had a mere half-dozen Thai attorneys with them. No matter what they presented, the barrage of objections raised by the other side was sustained and all their evidence was ruled inadmissible.

Finally, without any fanfare that Martin was aware of, the judge rose and left the courtroom.

The other attorneys packed their briefcases and left also.

Martin stared at the empty judge's chair.

"That's it?"

"No. That's *it* for today. We return in ninety days. "

Martin scowled.

"The judge was very clear that the evidence was not admitted and the guilty parties are already incarcerated…I told you this would be a long, frustrating experience."

Martin looked at Ben. "He was bought, Ben. It was obvious."

"He may have been influenced, that's certainly possible."

"You witnessed the same comedy of errors that I did."

"Let's go outside."

There was a small group of reporters waiting. A half-dozen microphones were pointed at Ben and Martin as they emerged.

Ben put himself between Martin and the press, but Martin put a hand on his shoulder. "Don't, Ben. Let me talk to them."

They asked Martin questions in Thai, expecting one of the attorneys to translate. They were quite surprised when Martin answered in perfect Thai.

"Khun Larue, what happened to your son?"

"He was a victim. A victim of negligence. He never should have died."

"There are three men in prison now—convicted of complicity in the death of your son. Does that bring you any satisfaction?"

"No. Not at all. The trials of those men were not public, and I have no idea of their actual role. But in any event, my attorneys and I are trying to get justice. Four men died, two others were seriously injured. We want the property developers to admit and accept their guilt. If proper safety procedures had been in place and enforced, my son and the other three would be here today."

"Khun Larue, what are you asking for from Khun Vithiya? How much money?"

"I have not asked for any money. Only justice. An admission of guilt would be enough for me."

———

In the car, Ben was quiet. Martin was wound up.

"We were talking in court about the judge being obviously influenced. I am a wealthy man. If that's what it takes, I can offer *influence* also."

Ben studied Martin a few moments before speaking. "Martin, Vithiya Sarawat's name will never appear in court. And you cannot challenge him financially. He could buy and sell you a hundred times and not feel it one bit. We have to find a weak spot…something that we can use to our advantage."

"I assume you're working on that."

"I am."

"Good. So am I."

———

"How is this going to work?"

The professor had just put the girl to bed in a ground-floor bedroom suite whose windows were barred and barricaded. She had been rendered unconscious by Ramonne and, for all intents and purposes, appeared to be having a nice, relaxing slumber. Except—the bedroom door was locked from the outside.

"I'm just starting to figure that out."

Ramonne didn't seem to be disturbed that they would now have an unwanted houseguest. He actually appeared to be going out.

"Oh, no. You can't just leave her with me."

"I'm only going out for little while. I'll be back before dawn."

"Of course you will. But will she still be asleep?"

Ramonne opened the door and stared back at the professor. "Of course she will."

He slammed the door and left.

The professor decided it would probably be wise if he used the stolen van to lay in some provisions for their new houseguest. So he ventured off to Villa Market and bought triple the normal household items he'd already laid in for himself and the master.

The master, of course, required no food, so his meager diet was easily attended to in his weekly forays. But now the professor loaded up on sanitary items, soaps, shampoos, toiletries—as well as all manner of frozen, canned, and baked goods, bottled water, beer—who knew what she drank—whiskey, white wine, and sodas.

He returned just after 1:00 a.m. and filled the fridge freezer pantry and guest toilet. He then parked the stolen van a few blocks away, being careful to look for the ever-present closed circuit cameras that Bangkok was now infatuated with.

Satisfied there were none, he returned to the fortress and settled in to await his master's return.

As usual, it was about an hour before dawn when the vampire returned. He was in an agitated state, his eyes glowing red.

The professor knew better than to say anything, and sat rock still.

The vampire moved to the massive steel door to his lair and entered. Within moments it slammed shut.

The professor sat very alone in silence, as outside the faint glow of false dawn broke.

That went well. He sighed to himself and opened a bottle of brandy.

———

The next day, the professor improvised. After all, he was a *doctor*. When he arose, he knocked softly on the guestroom door. No response, so he unlocked and opened it.

The girl, as promised, was still asleep.

He cautiously approached her and did a few simple examinations. Pulse, blood pressure.

All fairly normal.

He was prepared to give her a mild sedative, but instead he laid out a simple restorative meal on her bedside table. Oranges, a pitcher of water, fresh muffins. And quietly left and locked the door.

———

"My dear. How are you?"

Ramonne sat in the chair next to Juliette's bed.

She looked him dead in the eye.

"Who the fuck are you?"

"Well…that's rather direct. My name is Ramonne Delacroix."

"Ahhh. *Francais.*"

"*Oui, mademoiselle.* Let me apologize for the fact that we appear to be sequestering you here."

"It does appear like that."

"You must understand that my 'employer,' Monsieur Larue, wishes to protect you at all costs."

"Protect me?"

"Yes. You see, you are the only impartial witness to his son's death."

"Ah. So that's what this is. Witness protection."

"In a way. Yes."

"Why? Who is the threat?"

"Let's just say that there are very large corporate players involved who would like the death of Monsieur Larue's son to be forgotten sooner rather than later."

She mulled this over for a minute.

"You're the one who was watching me."

"I did observe you for a bit, yes."

"Then you know…I have *needs*."

"I think we can accommodate those—if that's absolutely necessary."

"If you want to keep me here quietly, waiting for that special day when I appear on the witness stand, then I suggest you *take care* of my needs."

13

March

Honesty dealt a crushing blow.

Last week, as the dust settled and work resumed at the site on Soi Langsuan where construction materials fell Christmas Eve and killed four and left two more in hospital, the Thai bureaucracy trundled out the same old incredibly insensitive mantra—"the families will be compensated"—as if that were the top priority when four people are crushed to death by a slab of concrete. How much longer can we tolerate the callous disregard for human life by the greedy corporate vultures molding our city's skyline with their endless supply of money-laundered condos?

Two key national figures for worker safety have assured that state compensation is forthcoming for those injured, and the families of those killed in the accident. But who is to be held responsible? Police have not released any names of the rumored three employees quickly incarcerated. It is known that one was the crane operator. It is the opinion of this newspaper that this is just business as usual, as the authorities do whatever is necessary to sidestep the contractor who is rightly (ir)responsible and should pay dearly for this desecration.

Martin put the paper down. He thought about Prakasan, the man who wrote the piece. His father was born in Calcutta and joined his family's migration to Thailand shortly after World War II. They settled in Bangkok's Pahurat district, a large fabric market adjacent to Chinatown. Prakasan was born in 1955 in the newly developed Indian center known as Nana. As a teenager he hustled the American GIs on Sukhumvit, until one day Martin's father saw something in the dark-skinned boy and gave him a job as a copy boy with his newly formed *Bangkok Times*—rival to the other English-language newspaper in Thailand, the *Bangkok Post*.

As the twentieth century ended, Prakasan was managing editor. In 2014, with his father's sudden death, Martin inherited the bulk of the company. Martin's younger brother inherited half, but, as a functioning alcoholic, he wisely ceded control to his older brother.

Martin allowed the various publishing entities to continue doing business with virtually their same staff. He had watched through the years as Prakasan had rightfully earned his position as managing editor.

He hoped that Prakasan didn't feel he needed to write such an editorial out of loyalty. He soon abandoned that thought. Prakasan had proved to be the most honest and unbiased newsman he had ever encountered.

In the current climate of "fake news" and incessant bullying of the press, the *Bangkok Times* had held its own, through coups and protests, giving an unbiased view on activities, political or royal, in the City of Angels.

Buoyed by the editorial, Martin decided it was time to try and resume a daily routine.

He changed into his gym clothes and told Areeya he was going to work out.

She kissed him and smiled to herself. *I just might get my husband back.*

The gym in Martin's building was on the floor below. Martin

had a small version—treadmill, exercycle, weights—in his apartment, but he enjoyed coming down and absorbing the energy of the youthful fitness buffs.

Martin normally had regular sessions with Khun Mal, a personal trainer. He had neglected these for the past three weeks. There was an air of surprise when he appeared at the entry.

"Khun Martin." He was greeted by the head female trainer, Jaew. "How good to see you."

"You, too. Is Khun Mal available?"

"I'm sorry. He's with a client. Can I suggest a substitute?"

"Certainly."

The gym was packed. It was high season. The apartment building was full with permanent residents and those owners who came from cold climates just for the winter months.

Jaew looked around and then shrugged her shoulders. "I'm available."

Martin smiled. "Perfect."

Jaew put Martin through a strenuous one-and-a-half-hour session that left him exhausted and sweating. He thanked her and then stripped off his shirt, rinsed in the outdoor shower, and fell into the cantilevered pool.

———

He appeared back at the apartment two hours after he left. He wore a white robe and his hair was damp. Areeya ruffled his damp hair.

"Feel better?"

"Yes. I do."

She hugged him to her. "We'll get through this. You know we will."

They kissed long and hard. Then he took her hand and walked her to the bedroom.

SARAWAT COMMUNICATIONS.

The name was emblazoned in silver neon atop the sixty-story slick glass rectangle, and in bronze four meters high at the entrance.

At the very top was a helicopter pad and a sleek black Sikorsky helicopter. The two-story windows in the penthouse floor below it were lit with a soft warm glow.

Across the street, from atop a construction crane, Ramonne watched as a large man in an expensive suit emerged from a solid gold door and crossed the elaborate living area where two bodyguards and a young woman in a bright-red dress awaited.

Vithiya Sarawat.

The vampire had been out of commission for nine years, but even so, he recognized the surname. The family was one of the most powerful in Thailand, involved in businesses—media, real estate, telecommunications, and oil—that kept them at the top of the *Fortune* 500. They had parlayed this empire into the halls of government and now held several powerful seats in the newly elected parliament. All this while—rumor had it—their hands were busy getting dirty in the lucrative drugs and arms trades.

Martin had his reasons for wanting to encounter him—but so did Ramonne. He had suspicions that, somehow, this man, a known enemy of Ping Narong, had something to do with the Russian in Phuket. Most likely, there would be extraordinary violence when Ramonne would attempt to encounter him. This was a man who was protected by security like a head of state.

He needed to figure out how to get to him when he was alone—which was probably never.

The time was about midnight, and Ramonne had been observing the penthouse for about three hours. Although Vithiya was the chairman of several companies that bore his name, Ramonne had found no evidence that he ever occupied the offices in those less imposing corporate headquarters. Not that it would have made much difference to the vampire. His comings and goings in the daytime were of little or no concern to him. He would not be able to encounter him in the daylight hours.

As for the seat that he recently occupied in the parliament, that was the most fortified building—outside of the Royal Palace—in Thailand. Meetings often stretched into the night, and were followed by lavish banquets. Ramonne had surveyed it already, and dismissed any attempt to breach its security as folly.

This was where they would meet. Sixty stories up, Ramonne was at a distinct advantage. His aerial skills allowed him to ascend sheer surfaces with the grace of a lizard, and sail through the air like a bat.

Vithiya Sarawat, his bodyguards, and the girl in the red dress—not his wife; Ramonne knew this without having to study the daily news—emerged from the rooftop elevator and entered the helicopter. It warmed up for a few minutes and then slowly ascended.

Ramonne watched it head west until it was merely a few blinking red and white lights in the night sky.

———

"Vithiya Sarawat."

Ping Narong sat in his regal, throne-like chair and studied Ramonne.

"What is your relationship?"

"He's my enemy. We are in the same business."

"What was his reaction when Somchai was killed?"

"I assume he was pleased. We both thought of Somchai as an enemy. If I took him out, or Vithiya took him out, it made no difference. We would both benefit. In fact, we were actually in the middle of a complicated arrangement. Dividing the territories. It seemed a stroke of good luck that I was the one who got to eliminate Somchai."

"How'd that work out?" Ramonne asked sarcastically.

"Not so well. Eventually…after Somchai was gone, Vithiya assassinated all of his secondary officers and took over his territory."

"That's not good for you."

"No. It's not."

"Why didn't you tell me about this?"

"Truthfully…I didn't want to involve you."

"Why not?"

"You told me what happened in Phuket. That man was Vithiya's man. I didn't want to start *that* war."

Ramonne considered this. "A war Ping Narong does not want to fight—I never thought I'd hear of that."

"I said I didn't want to *start* it. I didn't say I wouldn't fight it."

Ping leaned over and spoke softly to Ramonne. "You told me there was something strange in Phuket. You said you were fighting one of your own kind."

"I was."

Ping chewed on a slice of watermelon and frowned. "That's not good."

"You have no idea."

———

"She wants to go out."

"Where does she want to go?"

"I don't know. She just said she wants to go out."

The professor and the vampire stood outside the locked door to the girl's bedroom.

"Well, why didn't you take her for a walk?"

"What was I supposed to do? Put her on a leash?"

Ramonne thought about this. "No. I suppose not."

"Besides. She sleeps all day. And then she does her *medicine*. And then she passes out."

Ramonne shrugged. "I don't see the problem."

Professer Kaestle also shrugged in exasperation. "She's in a rut, master. She knows it. That's why today she screamed at me, 'I want to go *out*! Out of this fucking cage.'"

Ramonne had to smile at hearing the four letter word come out of the good professor's mouth.

"Where do you think she wants to go?"

"How should I know? I just feed her and clean her room."

It was about midnight. Ramonne was about to go hunting. But he supposed he could put that off for another night.

"All right. Open the door."

The professor unbolted the heavy lock and the door creaked open.

The girl was seated on an armchair next to the bed. Her unfinished meal was at the small dining table.

She smiled when she saw Ramonne. "Well, if it isn't my *master*."

The smile she gave to Ramonne startled him momentarily. "My dear. How are you this evening?"

"Bored. How long have I been your prisoner?"

"I don't like to think of you as a prisoner. You are my guest. I think this is a better habitat than the stinking hovel you were in when I brought you here."

"Yes. That was a low point. But normally I'm quite well taken care of. Young men, you know, tend to be easily manipulated."

"My friend's son being one of those?"

"I'm ready to discuss your friend's son whenever you are. But first, let me out. Please."

Her eyes pleaded but Ramonne saw it as an act. An act, however, he was prepared to pursue. Before he questioned this woman about Martin's son, he wanted to know more about her.

"All right." He extended a hand. "Come with me."

At first, Ramonne took the girl through the streets.

He spotted a man and a woman across a busy intersection having a heated discussion. The man gripped the woman's arm tightly, and she slapped him.

Ramonne pulled Juliette into a shadow, put a finger to her lips, and then allowed her to *hear* a lovers' quarrel. Their voices were muted to most by the traffic noise, but it was crystal clear to Ramonne and Juliet. She expressed mild surprise.

Then he upped the ante a bit by taking her to the Chao Phraya River. They sat on the bank and watched ferries and rice barges motoring slowly by—but soon the scene morphed into an ancient tableau of French and Portuguese frigates, their tall masts strung with lanterns to mark them for the many merchants who were bringing long rowboats loaded with barrels of whiskey and winsome Thai girls to entertain the sailors on board. Just as it was toward the end of the nineteenth century when Ramonne arrived in Bangkok.

Justine was now wide-eyed in wonder. She spoke to him in French. "*You are an ancient soul.*"

"I am," he replied.

"So am I."

At that moment, Ramonne knew that this woman and he had much...*much* in common.

"You should come with me to Paris. Let me *show* you the French Revolution."

As she said it...Ramonne saw it. He was in the Place de la Concorde, but not the magnificent plaza it is today. What he saw was a bloodthirsty horde massed around a raised stage where a giant guillotine came crashing down and a human head rolled forth to the cheers from the crowd.

For the first time he could remember, Ramonne was *amazed*. And then, without knowing he had done it, Ramonne took her on a hunt. He grabbed her hand. He walked hand-in-hand with the girl no more than five minutes before he saw a man with a knife glistening in the night. He was waiting outside a dimly-lit tavern.

Ramonne and the girl stepped out of the shadows, walking like lovers.

The man with the knife shifted his attention to them and followed. Within a half block, Ramonne spun around and picked the man up by the throat and sunk his teeth into the carotid artery.

Juliette stared in wide-eyed fascination.

————

Ramonne feasted on the would-be thief. The blood dripped from his lips as he looked up at the wide-eyed damsel. He had never known anyone to witness his acts of carnage without repulsion—except the female Kanchana, who he had virtually created. Even Martin, blinded by the powerful hallucinations he held over him with his mind manipulation, sometimes became repulsed when the bloodletting started in earnest.

But this young girl was merely fascinated; she stared as one would at a film star on a red carpet.

Ramonne felt selfish. If she was so uninhibited, perhaps she would like to participate—to enjoy the spoils—to *feast*.

He pointed to the blood flowing freely, and offered. But she demurely declined, as demurely as a debutante at a summer ball declining a dance.

"We don't feast on their blood."

"We?"

'Yes. We."

"Don't feast on blood?"

There was a long pause.

"I see there is much I need to know about you."

Juliette merely smiled.

"Enjoy your meal. And thank you for getting me out of the house."

———

Hemingway's was a two-story, open-courtyard bar and restaurant on Sukhumvit Soi 11. Unlike the fairly quiet Soi 8 on the other side of Sukhumvit, Soi 11 was an ever-expanding hubbub of restaurants, nightclubs, upmarket cafés, hotels, and anything else they could cram into its narrow two lanes.

Martin entered and quickly spotted Ben. He had a quiet table in the rear.

"Ben."

"Martin."

They met so frequently now, that this was all they needed to say as introduction. Martin sat down. A waiter placed a menu in front of him, and Martin politely pushed it aside. "Just coffee. Americano."

Ben, as usual, had file folders in front of him. But he didn't bother to open them.

"Martin. I have some confidential information on your case. The matriarch of the Sarawat family inquired about you."

Martin did not know what to say, so he waited.

"She asked their family attorney, 'What is the Thai family name of the *farang* that is threatening us?'"

"*Threatening* them?"

"It's a figure of speech."

Martin waited for the response.

"The attorney said your wife's family's name, Boonsong. And she merely waved a hand in dismissal saying, 'They are not of significance.'"

Martin was stunned. "My wife? Her family name means *nothing*?"

"Unfortunately, yes. That's how they see you."

"How they see me?"

"You're a *farang*. They've already dismissed you."

Martin was furious.

Ben poured a glass of water from a pitcher and offered it to Martin.

Martin swept his hand across the table, sending the glass flying. "They do not know who they are dealing with."

Ben set the pitcher down.

"Martin. Calm down. I told you this would be difficult. We need to be patient."

Martin stood up.

"Ben. You're my dear friend. And my attorney. *You* be patient. Be persistent. Do everything you can to get justice. But I can wait no longer."

———

The professor was trying to wean himself from the habit of waiting for the master to return. It was never more than an hour before dawn when the vampire would make his appearance.

The professor had certain responsibilities in the daytime that required him to function like a normal person. Bills to pay, the master's various tastes to attend to, as well as the management of the house.

But he felt that his main responsibility was the master himself, and that meant reassuring himself that he returned safely. Lord knows how many times in their long relationship that they were under attack by all manner of assailants intent on obliterating the vampire and, by association, the professor as well.

Consequently, the professor had taken to sleeping on the massive leather couch in the seldom-used living room. He had a perfectly comfortable bedroom suite on the second floor, but if he was there, he would not be aware when *he* came home.

Once the master was safely ensconced in his crypt, the

professor could indulge himself with several hours of deep sleep in a real bed.

Hence, he was just starting to slumber on the couch when, to his surprise, the master and the girl burst through the door. Completely oblivious of him. Entwined, rapturous, their lips locked, their hips cocked and fully loaded. They breezed across the entry to the girl's room. Ramonne effortlessly picked up the girl and carried her through the door. He slammed the door shut with his hips.

Realizing he had just been made redundant, he wrapped his blanket around himself and trudged upstairs.

———————

Nearly two centuries of carnal knowledge had made Ramonne Delacroix quite the cocksman. He had yet to meet the woman that he could not satisfy. But Juliette Dorval was something else.

Again, she reminded him of Kanchana, the female vampire that he "created" after the woman who embodied her original form demanded it in return for having resurrected him. She had dallied with the necromancer's arts, but didn't have the black heart for the killing. She eventually asked Ramonne to release her, and he did.

But years later, in retreat at Siem Reap, in the shadow of Angkor and growing bored, he drew her back to him. This proved to be both fantastic and fatalistic.

The sex was fantastic.

But again, she was not a hunting partner, and she put him in jeopardy. So he destroyed her once and for all. With deep regret.

But this vixen…

She was amazing. His inner clock told what time it was, but he knew he had to be careful. With this one, he could lose all sense of time, and could place himself in jeopardy as the sun rose.

She appeared to be in her late twenties. Maybe younger. But

the drug use had given a hard edge to her natural beauty. But Ramonne realized he was being taken in by the same mysterious façade that *he* presented to all who met him. Still appearing to be in his mid- to late thirties, a bit roguish, the ever-growing shock of gray in his longish hair, he, in truth, was now close to one hundred and ninety years old.

He vowed to unlock all of this wonderful creature's mysteries.

They had flown back to the house using the rooftops. The girl had been completely overwhelmed. She had never experienced anything like it. This intrigued him even further. He made several attempts to find out what she was, but each time she placed a finger to his lips and simply said "Later."

Now, in the arena of the bedroom, he was simply concentrating on his performance. Ramonne was as vain as any mortal. If not more so.

He had power over women that he learned in over one hundred and seventy years of practice. He had positions that none, except perhaps the most experienced whore, had even heard of—much less tried.

Yet, to Juliette, it was seemingly nothing new.

So he upped his game a notch…and she liked it. So much so that she responded in kind. Violently wresting control from him, and submitting him to *her* will.

Momentarily caught off guard, Ramonne actually found himself going over the edge. This woman was pushing him to an early climax!

Grabbing her by her ankles, he flipped her over so she was facing him. He then reinserted himself, pulling her legs together and lifting her ankles straight up while he thrust hard. She stared at him in shock and pleasure.

And then they both exploded in rapture together. This triggered several minutes of rapturous moaning, and then they fell back on the bed and looked at each other.

Simultaneously they laughed out loud and howled.

———

Upstairs, the professor was just falling asleep when the ruckus below shook the house to its foundations. This was followed by a loud and unholy wail.

"Well, I never." He pulled a pillow over his ears and tried to ignore the commotion below.

14

April

"Where is he?"

"I suspect you know where he is. He's asleep."

Martin was on the phone with the professor. Ramonne had forbidden a cellphone in his house because of its multiple tracking devices. But the professor had arranged to keep the landline installed that came with the house, and paid the bill several years in advance.

"I realize that. I need to meet him."

"Of course."

Martin waited.

"You're not telling me something."

"Excuse me?"

"The girl. What's happening with her?"

"Nothing is happening with her."

Martin waited. Again…nothing.

"Jesus. Talking with you is like talking to a wall. Tell him to meet me tonight. Midnight at Smalls."

"I will, sir."

————

Smalls. A three-story bar and nightclub in the Suan Plu area of tiny streets off Sathorn Road. New home to Bangkok's regular crew of old-hand expats. Its owner, David Jacobson, was known as the "Godfather" of expat nightlife in Southeast Asia. He opened his first nightclub, the Q Bar, in Saigon in 1992, following its success with a wildly successful nightclub of the same name in Bangkok in 1999. When Q Bar had run its course in Bangkok's fickle nightlife scene, Jacobson scaled down his operations and opened Smalls.

Casual, hip, it reeked of eccentric old-world grace. The drinks, Martinis, Mai Tais, and shots of absinthe were poured by extremely talented mixologists.

Martin enjoyed a light meal at the downstairs bar with Jacobson, and then climbed the circular stairs to the rooftop. There was a jazz trio playing, and Martin took a seat on a sofa at the roof's edge.

A young diva was singing. Martin thought she was perfect. Her sultry voice captured the Billie Holiday piece she was performing, and the trio supporting her did the same.

They signaled they were taking a break, and left the stage.

It was then that Ramonne appeared.

"She's good, yes?"

Martin smiled. "Very good."

Ramonne had a glass of wine. He placed it on the table next to Martin's martini, and sat in a chair. He was facing the shimmering city skyline behind Martin. He smiled.

"This city. It never stops changing. Never stops growing."

"Unfortunately, yes."

They sipped their drinks in silence.

"Vithiya Sarawat. Have you met him?"

"No. He won't meet me."

"I can meet him."

"Are you sure?"

"Yes. I believe he wants something from me."

"What?"

"It has to do with the situation in Phuket."

"The *other one* you encountered there?"

Ramonne nodded.

"What do you think he wants?"

"I believe, to control them."

"*Them?*"

"I believe there are more, and they work for Vithiya. He must know who I am, and realizes I'm the only one who can stop it."

Many minutes passed. The moon rose over the distant river. They sipped their drinks, lost in thought.

"What about the girl?"

Ramonne was careful with his answer. "She is interesting. I don't know everything yet, but it seems we have some things in common."

At this Martin was shocked. "I have never heard you say that about anyone."

Ramonne looked as innocent as a one hundred and ninety year-old vampire could. "It seems she is also a very old soul."

"Really? How so?"

"As yet I have no idea."

"Why do you say such a thing?"

"We went out."

"You went *out?*"

"Yes. She complained about being locked in the room, so I took her out."

Martin was afraid what the answers would be, but still he had many questions. "And?"

"We went down by the river."

"Oh no. You didn't?"

"Yes."

"Why?"

"Why not? It's a history lesson."

"Yes. But it blows people's minds."

"Well, it didn't blow *hers*. She simply told me to come to Paris sometime and take a walk with her. Then she let me see a few frames of the French Revolution…if you know what I mean."

Martin was aghast. "So she's a—"

"No." Ramonne cut him off. "Definitely not."

"Then what is she?"

"I don't know yet. But definitely an old soul."

"How old?"

"I'm guessing one hundred and fifty years. Or more."

"Jesus."

Martin finished his martini in one shot and motioned to the waitress. Then he stared at the vampire. "I simply wanted you to babysit her. Keep her available for the trial. Maybe, just maybe, find out a little more about her."

"Which I did."

"No. You realized she was some kind of paranormal entity, and you seduced her."

"I resent that."

"Fine. Resent it. It's a fact." He suddenly had a scary thought. "She can go out in the daytime, can't she? I've seen her in the daytime."

"Yes. I told you. She's not one of us. But this doesn't change anything. We have her under our control. She and I have just become…a little *close*."

Martin shook his head. His drink arrived, along with another glass of wine for Ramonne. Martin took it from the waiter and nearly finished it in one gulp.

"Right now my problem is with this Vithiya character. He seems to consciously be in control of substandard construction projects throughout the city. Bribes to local authorities and politicians keep the projects going. When there is an accident, the same thing happens in the court. These 'accidents' kill and maim his workers and innocent pedestrians, but the human lives are inconsequential."

Martin finished his drink and got up and started to leave.

"Unfortunately, one of his victims was *my son*."

Ramonne slowly nodded. "I understand."

15

The private elevator ascended quietly to the sixtieth floor. The bronze doors, inlaid with onyx, opened smoothly and two security guards stepped into the hall. They each wore a Kevlar vest and carried a Glock 9 mm pistol. They swept the hallway and traversed the short distance into the penthouse.

"All clear," the first guard spoke into a microphone.

Vithiya Sarawat entered the room, accompanied by more security guards, a secretary, and a butler.

Vithiya removed his suit jacket and handed it to his butler. As he did, the high-backed leather chair behind the rosewood desk slowly spun so that it faced the room. As it moved, six gun barrels were trained on it.

Ramonne—seated in the chair—was unfazed. Vithiya motioned to the guards to put down their weapons. Cautiously they lowered their guns but kept them at the ready.

Ramonne spoke softly: "Do you know who I am?"

"Yes." Vithiya smiled. "Ramonne Delacroix."

"Do you know what I am?"

"Yes. *Phi dib*…One of the *undead*."

Ramonne nodded. "Vampires…You know these men cannot harm me. I could kill all of them in an instant."

"Yes."

"Then I suggest you dismiss them, for you and I need to talk."

Vithiya spoke to one man—obviously the leader. The man resisted at first, but soon all of the guards, the butler, and the secretary retreated and closed the heavy penthouse door. Vithiya locked the door and turned to Ramonne, who was now at the window gazing into the night sky.

"How many of those tall buildings are yours?"

"To be honest, I don't actually know. At least a dozen."

"I've lived in this city for over a hundred and fifty years and I barely recognize it today."

He turned back and faced Vithiya. He studied his face.

"You don't fear me…Why is that?"

"Why should I fear you?"

"All mortals should fear me. You are my *prey*."

Vithiya motioned to the window. "You have a whole city full of prey. You don't need me." He went to a smooth teak bookcase, pressed a button, and a fully stocked bar appeared. "Can I offer you a drink?"

Ramonne nodded. "Wine. Red."

Ramonne continued to study the man as he opened the bottle and poured two glasses. "You've been expecting me."

"I have." He handed the glass to Ramonne.

"I have only met four vampires in my long time on this planet. I am very careful to make sure I take the life of my victims. This deprives them of the curse. It is only if you take their blood and let them *survive* that they then become vampires themselves."

"Who were they?"

"One was an ancient Chinese who gave me the curse. I eventually destroyed him. One was a jealous man whose woman I had taken. We fought and he escaped—wounded. Eventually we met again. A third was a female *I* created. I was lonely and she asked for it. Unfortunately she had no taste for the killing, and I destroyed her."

Ramonne paused and turned to the window again. "And one I just recently met in Phuket. And I destroyed him."

"The Russian. Dimitri Kirilov."

"Yes. You know about that?"

"He worked for me. They all do."

"*They?*"

"There are a half-dozen of them—all Russian. They stay in Phuket and run errands for me. They blend in there. No one seems to notice them."

As Vithiya was telling him this, Ramonne was *seeing* it. He saw muscular Russian men in a discotheque. Strobe lights flashing, rhythmic music thumping, and tattooed women in skimpy bikinis. *Yes. They do blend in.*

"Goran—the coven's leader—told me about you. He mentioned an ancient manuscript and something called the Oracle. Apparently the Japanese Black Dragons and the Russians are comrades in arms. I remembered the stories of you working for Ping—you were a legend. And then you disappeared."

"And now I'm back."

"Yes. And for taking out Dimitri, I thank you. These men, these Russians, are out of control. They're supposed to launder money for me, move narcotics, do the odd hit. Just normal business. Instead, they're going on a rampage. They have left a trail of floating bodies and blood-drained corpses. Across the island. Initially I thought Dimitri was the only rogue. But he was just the first. Their leader, Goran, hasn't reported to me once since he took over."

"So what would you have me do?"

"Kill them. Kill them all."

———

Three vehicles traveled in a convoy the next day heading south from Bangkok. In the lead was a civilian Humvee. Inside, specially constructed compartments held the armaments of a small militia. Its glossy black paint job concealed the heavy metal plating. The passengers, posing as senior Thai government officials on a holiday lark, were a half-dozen of Vithiya's private guard.

The second vehicle, an RV, held the professor and Juliette. It was pretty much what it looked like—a home on wheels. Shower, toilet, cooking facilities, beds. Under the floorboards, however, was more weaponry. Extremely unconventional. Swords, battle axes, throwing knives.

The last vehicle was a sleek black Mercedes Sprinter van—customized to accommodate Ramonne the way Ping's Toyota Granvia had been. It was protected from prying eyes by diplomatic plates and the police uniforms of the men in front. In the center, it carried Ramonne's coffin. His *comfort zone*. He never got a better day's sleep than in a coffin. This particular one was his favorite. He'd had it for fifty years. He'd slept rough, burrowed in a forest or in a damp cave, when on the run from Cambodia to Thailand. He'd slept in cheap beds when he first arrived in Bangkok, and felt no pain. But he slept so well when he first slept in a coffin, so he maintained the tradition.

The convoy crossed the Sarasin Bridge at dusk and sailed through the checkpoint without incident. It was dark when they pulled into a small park shaded by casuarina trees along a white sandy beach. The professor killed the RV's engine and stepped out onto the sand. He slid the door of the Mercedes van open and waited. Shortly, the coffin's lid was raised and Ramonne arose. He stretched and climbed out gracefully. The professor extended a hand, but it was unnecessary.

"Where are we?"

"Phuket, master."

He stepped out of the van, nodding to the men who stood at attention alongside the professor.

"Where's the girl?"

"In the RV."

"What is an *RV*?"

"A recreational vehicle. What we used to call motor homes."

"A *trailer*…yes?"

"Basically. Motorized vehicles have been evolving rapidly. Soon they will drive themselves."

"Good. Then I won't need you."

"Sir?"

"A *joke*. Come on. Let's see our little beauty."

The professor entered the vehicle and gently called her name. "Miss Juliette?" No answer.

Ramonne looked to the beach, and there she was.

He joined her. The stars glowed in the deep-blue night sky. Tiny luminescent fish and plankton rolled with each incoming wave, causing the surf to glow.

"It's beautiful."

"Yes. It is."

She turned to him. "It's been eons, literally, since I've been to the sea."

"Consider this your long-overdue seaside vacation—with the added bonus of a chance to massacre a coven of Russian vampires."

"My darling…you spoil me."

She kissed him, with a hundred years of passion. He reciprocated.

The professor stepped aside as Ramonne picked her up and carried her into the RV and shut the door.

———

Ramonne insisted they all stay at Andara, the beautiful five-star resort he had stayed at on his first trip to the island. They needed to rent a very large villa that would accommodate them all and their vehicles.

The complex they took over resembled Angkor Wat, with its steep staircases that took one from the master bedroom, to guest rooms one through four, kitchens one and two, the pool, and the basement gym and sauna.

Ramonne enjoyed leaping to the various levels, and the militia had no problem with the stairs, but the professor attempted to keep up with the vampire, huffing and puffing all the while, until he finally declared that the enclosed entry adjacent to the parking lot would be his domain during their stay. Ramonne laughed at this as his coffin was carried downstairs and locked inside the master suite. Strict instructions had been made that during their stay, no maids or other household help was to enter the premises.

It was midnight by the time all were settled. Ramonne gathered them together.

"All right. Let's go meet them." He decided that tonight it would be just he and Juliette that would make contact. The rest would stay close by. Within reach. If need be. And he told the professor he could stay home.

Café del Mar, 1:00 a.m.

Ramonne and Juliette looked perfectly decadent enough. She was in a form-hugging single piece of fabric that clung to her curves and revealed more skin than it covered. He wore an open white shirt that revealed his perfect physique. There was one flaw in their appearance. Neither of them looked like they had seen the sun in a long, long time. This made them stand out from the suntanned, sunburnt, and just plain barbecued beach crowd.

But they weren't the only ones. They were spotted immediately by a blond Adonis with no shirt, and a stoned redhead attempting not to fall over while dancing. The Adonis whispered something to a muscle-bound skinhead with twin teenage girls.

The Adonis immediately left the skinhead and approached Ramonne. "Ah. You have come back."

Ramonne ignored the remark.

"You must be Goran."

"Yes. Dimitri was my friend."

"He was a pig."

The skinhead rushed at Ramonne but Goran grabbed him by the neck and pulled him back. "No. You know better. Not here."

Ramonne did not want to back off, but in looking around, he realized the entire place was filled with Russians. Men and women. Most were probably not vampires. But at least a half-dozen were. The blood and mayhem that such a battle would inflict on those others on the dance floor was unimaginable.

So, Ramonne also backed off. He took Juliette's arm and led her onto the dance floor. He pulled her to him and they danced a sultry samba that was in concert with the music.

"Ahhh…you truly *are* insane. I knew I liked you for a reason."

They danced while a half-dozen Russian vampires watched.

———

Back at Andara, they made love again. Ramonne had not had such a passionate partner in a quarter-century.

Afterwards they drank, talked, and planned. She also had experience fighting. As she described her fights, he saw them, and he was amazed at how she wielded her makeshift weapons —pots and pans, pitchforks, hoes, axes. He promised to educate her in the swords he had brought. This excited her immensely, and shortly they were entwined again.

Ramonne called a meeting about an hour before dawn, waking the professor and half the team. They slept in shifts so as to be on the alert for an attack day or night. Ramonne's instructions stated that obviously the Russians had a group of servants who performed their daily tasks for them. He wanted to make contact with them and inform them that it was Vithiya's intention to make peace. All Ramonne desired was a simple meeting to negotiate the terms.

Vithiya had given them the address of the last known location of *his* Russians. It was a villa on a hillside overlooking Surin Beach—once party central for the entire island, but in a supreme case of foot-shooting the network of restaurants, bars, and the number-one beach club in the world for four years running, were demolished by the government for no apparent reason. It now lay vacant, stagnant, and abandoned—awaiting its next reincarnation, which, in modern-day Phuket, was never far away.

Since Vithiya had had no communication from the Russians in the past month, he had no further clues to their whereabouts. No GPS links. No digital footprints. So, while the vampire slept, the professor, Vithiya's sergeant-at-arms Nanork, his lieutenant Krung, and two others, piled into the Hummer and drove up the winding cliff-side road to the Surin Satay Villas. They reached the villas after a terrifying ten-minute climb. How on earth any government could allow the construction of such a steep and hazardous road, puzzled the professor.

The Surin Villas were much less guarded than the Andara, but this allowed its guests the luxury of cavorting without prying eyes. Its remote location meant anything went—prostitution, drugs, gambling, and, most likely, murder.

There was no one present as far as they could tell. No vehicles. No sign of life. Nanork motioned to his men and they all drew their weapons. He led them up the stairs to the front door. It was locked. A buzzer rang without any answer.

He stayed behind a high, rough stone wall and led them to the rear of the property, where the various decks jutted out over the steep hillside. They were level with a massive swimming pool. Nanork motioned that he would go first. Holding his automatic in front of him, Nanork cautiously approached the pool in a crouch. After ten meters, he stood up. His gun hand dropped to his side. He motioned for the others to come forward, and he slipped his pistol back in its holster.

Floating in the pool, like Japanese blowfish, were a half-dozen bloated human corpses. They were all Thai and middle-aged except for one young woman and a little boy. Nanork said sadly, "I think we've found the staff." He said to Krung, "Check all the rooms, but I doubt we'll find anything."

The professor looked away from the gruesome sight, and, to his surprise, saw Juliette standing behind him. "Madame. I didn't know you were with us?"

"Of course, where else would I be?"

Nanork ignored Juliette and addressed the professor. "You see what we are up against here?"

"Yes. I've seen this many times."

"Madame?" Nanork looked at Juliette. He expected a show of emotion.

Instead she walked slowly around the pool. She came to a large woman floating face down. She grabbed her ankles and spun her so that the black eyes stared right at her. She stared back.

Nanork watched this strange occurrence until Juliette walked on—continuing to connect with each corpse.

Krung was back. "Nothing, sir. Just this."

It was a business card. For another villa. Nanork took the card. "This was not an accident. This was left for us." He told Krung to get the men ready to leave.

He walked back to the pool and stood beside Juliette. "Madame. We need to leave."

Juliette was bending down to look at the boy. She smiled before she stood. "Of course."

The Black Pearl Villa was situated midway up Millionaire Mile between Kamala and Patong. The first of many multi-million-dollar villas, it was built on a former jungle path that wound along the seaside atop spectacular cliffs with spectacular views.

Andara, where Ramonne and crew were camped, was at the head of this now magnificent assemblage of ostentation. It should rightly be called "Billionaire Mile" for—as the prices continued to soar—they were the only ones who could afford to live there now. Nanork stopped at Andara and picked up the rest of his crew.

The Black Pearl was unique in that it consisted of one—and only one—very enormous villa complex. Guardhouse, multiple pools, guest dwellings of course—all in one huge fortress.

The Hummer approached and was immediately stopped by a Thai behemoth in a tight uniform. Nanork did the talking. He had rehearsed a speech that he delivered convincingly. He said he had been sent from Bangkok to provide extra security for the new Russian occupants of the villa. This rattled the guard, for it implied that this rather official-looking Thai knew that the villa was occupied by Russians.

However, that still wasn't enough to get through the gate.

That was when Juliette appeared. "Goran...I'm here for him."

This they understood. The gate was opened and the Hummer was allowed to pass. But when the gate closed there now stood six guards. Nanork and Krung opened the door and four more of Vithiya's men stepped out.

A standoff.

Juliette walked to the pool, where she found a half-dozen assorted whores in various stages of disarray. After a short while she decided that nothing could be accomplished here in the daytime. She took one of the girls aside and asked her, "Who is with Goran?" The girl pointed to the stoned redhead from the previous evening. Juliette approached her. "Darling, we need to talk."

The girl looked at Juliette like she was from Mars. "Who needs to talk?"

"You and I."

———

Ramonne awoke at dusk and climbed out of his coffin. He was alone. He went up the stairs. The RV was there but the Sprinter and the Hummer were gone. He wasn't sure what to make of this.

He dressed casually and walked down the hill to the restaurant and poolside bar. He ordered a reasonable Bordeaux and amused himself listening to the conversations in the restaurant. The languages were no problem to him. He understood them all. What he found amusing was that they were mostly concerned with matters of short-term consequence.

"Will it rain and ruin our vacation?"

"The stock exchange was strong today—but what about tomorrow?"

And, of course, all the numerous attempts at seduction.

Suddenly he *heard* the Hummer. He got up and paid the bill. He went out the back way and leapt up the hills rather than wait for a golf cart.

At the villa he was met by Nanork, Krung, and Juliette.

"What did you learn?"

"We followed Vithiya's directions to the house on the steep cliff. There was no one alive there. Mostly household staff, and one child. Floating in the pool. A quick search turned up a clue that led us to another villa—actually a fortress—further up this road. I suspect it was not chance that led us there. They meant for us to know where they are."

Ramonne waited for him to continue.

"We went there and would have been unable to enter if it hadn't been for Ms. Juliette."

Ramonne looked to her. She curtseyed. He laughed.

"The security staff wanted nothing to do with us. But she went to the pool and spent an hour or so with their whores. She ingratiated herself with Goran's mistress, and we now have a plan to meet them at the 9th Floor restaurant at ten o'clock tonight."

Ramonne fumed. "Did you not understand that I wished to meet them at a secluded place—like their villa? Rather than a populated establishment like where we were last night?"

"Yes, of course I understood. But this is a very private restaurant, occupying the ninth floor of a building overlooking Patong. I think we can be in control of the situation there."

Ramonne looked in Nanork's eyes. "You do…do you?"

"Yes. I seriously believe this is the place to meet. If we met at their villa, we'd have to deal with their entire security force."

"Which, you realize, I could take care of by myself."

This took Nanork back a bit, but he recovered. "We can go to the restaurant now and be ready for them."

"Then I suggest we do that."

———

Nine o'clock.

The Hummer and the RV parked as close to the entrance as their size permitted. Nanork and his crew got two crates out of the Hummer, and a smaller metal case from the RV. The professor stayed downstairs while the rest of the group split up to ride the tiny elevators.

The entrance to 9th Floor restaurant looked like any apartment building in Patong. Stained floors and walls, stray dogs, a minimart, a small office selling insurance. Two ancient elevators ascended very slowly to the ninth floor—the top floor.

Crammed in with Ramonne, Nanork, Krung, and Juliette on the first trip, was a blind woman and a Chihuahua. She found the fifth-floor button without help and wished them all a good night. The elevator stopped at each of the next three floors for no apparent reason. They seemed to be home to drug addicts, long-term low-budget expats, and some seedy-looking Thais.

When the building first opened thirty years ago, it was the tallest building in Patong. Since then it had been eclipsed by many taller, uninspired buildings, but none more decrepit-looking. However, when the elevator finally did arrive at the ninth floor and the doors opened—suddenly they were in a sophisticated version of Hugh Hefner's "Playboy After Dark" penthouse. Floor-to-ceiling windows overlooked a spectacular view from city to the sea.

Suitably impressed, Ramonne and Juliette stepped out of the elevator. They were met by the beautiful maître d' Khun Tuck. Khun Tuck was one of nine "Angels"—recruited as much for their good looks and long legs as their waitressing skills.

"Good evening. Do you have a reservation?"

Ramonne smiled and, without Khun Tuck knowing what had happened, she was under his spell. "We will be joining another party later." He surveyed the room. "But for now, we'd like that table near the back windows. There will be eight of us."

"Yes, sir. Certainly."

Ramonne spotted the large walk-in wine cabinet just to the left of the table he had chosen. "We have a few things to add to the wine cabinet."

"Of course."

Ramonne motioned to Nanork, and he and Krung brought the two oblong boxes into the room and placed them on the floor of the large wine cooler. No one paid them any attention. Ramonne told Nanork to open the boxes and make sure they were readily accessible.

The elevator pinged and four more of Vithiya's crew appeared, carrying a metal crate.

Ramonne seemed to have put the entire staff of Angels under his spell, as none of them challenged anything they did. They simply went about the business of setting up the table and taking drinks orders. Ramonne ordered several good bottles of red, and relaxed. The windows were open to the night sky, and a pleasant breeze drifted through the cavernous room.

Ten o'clock. The elevator pinged again and Goran and his coven of vampires appeared, along with their whores.

Khun Tuck showed them to the long table in the center of the room. Goran smiled at Ramonne. For the first time, Ramonne noticed a solid gold tooth in his upper palate.

The Angels opened several bottles of Beluga vodka and poured shots all around the table. Goran downed his and then picked up a bottle and walked to Ramonne's table.

He clinked the bottle with Ramonne's wine glass and downed a healthy slug of vodka. He wiped his mouth with the back of his sleeve. He spoke in Russian. *"What do you want?"*

Ramonne replied in English. He knew Goran would understand. "I want you to stop what you're doing."

Goran switched to English. "Oh? And what is that?"

"Killing innocents, for one thing."

"And you don't do that?"

"I try not to."

"Well, aren't you a *pussy*." Goran took another slug of vodka from the bottle.

"Vithiya sent you here to do a job. You've done it. Go home."

"I should go back to Russia because you want me to? Back to the long cold winters? I prefer it here."

"Then I'll send you back."

"You will send me back?"

"I will send you somewhere. Either back to Russia or to hell."

Goran swept Ramonne's wine bottle and glass off the table. They smashed on the floor. "Really? You would challenge me?"

Ramonne didn't bother to stand up. "Yes." He nodded to Nanork, who went into the wine cabinet with Krung. He then turned to Khun Tuck. Without exchanging a word, she gathered the Angels and hurried them into the kitchen. Goran's men stood up from the table. Their eyes began to glow, and animalistic sounds emanated from their throats.

Goran leapt at Ramonne, but Ramonne met the onrush with such force that Goran was knocked across the room. Ramonne put up his right hand, and Nanork tossed him a double-bladed broad axe. Instantly, Ramonne leaped atop the long table where Goran's men were gathered. With one mighty swing, he lopped off the head of the monster who stood at the head of the table.

Juliette watched wide-eyed as the head flew across the room, trailing blood over the table, and bounced on the floor. She stood and yelled to Nanork, "Arm me!"

Nanork flung a heavy sword to her. Surprisingly she was able to wield it without any problem. Ramonne leaped from the table and stood next to her.

"Sorry…we never got around to those lessons."

"Don't worry, darling. This feels just fine." Saying that, she plunged the blade through a long-haired beast that was about to sink his fangs in her.

"You have to cut off the head." Ramonne performed the coup de grâce, and another head rolled onto the floor with its corpse spraying a fountain of blood.

Nanork, Krung, and the other of Vithiya's men were blasting away with their pistols, their bullets merely annoyances to the vampires, two of whom decided to silence them. Ramonne yelled, "Use the blades! Cut off their heads." Krung was too late. One of the undead was upon him before he could reach the crate. He was dragged down screaming and writhing on the blood-soaked floor.

Nanork was luckier. He grabbed a smaller version of the broadsword that Juliette was wielding, and hacked away at the beast attacking him. The screams from the vampire were deafening but eventually the head was severed and joined the river of blood that was now covering the floor of the restaurant.

Unable to reach Nanork and get blades, the other four were

soon overrun. Ramonne tried to get to them but the table—and Goran—stood in the way. Nanork joined Ramonne and Juliette —helplessly listening to the dying screams of the men he had brought on this mission.

Goran smiled as his three remaining vampires joined him, their mouths red-rimmed with blood.

"Now, *pussy*, it's four of *us* and one of you."

He motioned and the three vampires leaped on the table. Ramonne smiled and swung his broad axe in a semi-circle, cutting off the feet of the vampire directly in front of him. Juliette got the idea, and did the same with her sword. Those two fell to the floor in front of Ramonne and Juliette. Ramonne swiftly lopped off the head of the one he struck, while Juliette did the same with hers.

"Correction. Two of you, two of us." He spoke to Nanork without turning his head. "Sorry, but Juliette is not exactly human. I'm not exactly sure what she is, but I think we're lucky, don't you?"

"Yes, sir. Very lucky."

Goran was clearly at the end of his rope. He motioned at the skinhead ghoul who was his last vampire standing. "Well…? Get them."

Goran pushed him and he fell onto Juliette's blade as it came sweeping up, slicing his head clean off in one stroke.

"Whoa." Ramonne cheered. "Bravo!"

Juliette bowed while Goran leaped to the windowsill. In a flash, he was out on the exterior of the building and heading for the roof.

Ramonne put his axe down and said to Nanork, "Give me your blade." Nanork handed it over.

Ramonne climbed onto the windowsill. "I suggest you check with your men. One or two of them may still be alive, in which case they can help you clean up this mess. Take one of the wooden crates and put the heads in it. Just the heads. Find a large trash bin in the street below, and move it under one of these windows. Throw the corpses out the window and into it. The rest—the staff can clean up. I'll instruct them, and then they'll forget we were here."

He looked at the whores. They were huddled in a corner, crying.

"And take *them* downstairs. Get them a cab."

With that, he climbed out the window.

———

Goran sat atop the building, leaning against a round air duct with a rusty TV antenna strapped to it. Spread before him was a glittering cityscape of one-way streets, maddening traffic, restaurants, bars, apartment buildings, shopping malls, hotels— four star and zero star—open-air markets, and the sea. A full moon reflected off the waves rolling ashore. Two massive cruise ships were anchored offshore.

Ramonne easily climbed the slick plaster-finished exterior, and stood on the tar-paper roof.

Goran didn't turn to look at him. He continued to stare straight ahead.

"How old are you?"

"How *old*?"

"Yes."

"About one hundred and ninety years, give or take a few."

"Almost two centuries. That's a nice long life."

"Well…I'm not really *alive*."

"You know what I mean."

"And you?"

"I was twenty-eight when I was *turned*. That was thirty years ago. I thought I was immortal."

"Under most circumstances you are."

"Dying at fifty-eight is hardly immortal."

Ramonne stood behind the vampire. "You should have kept a lower profile."

"You think so…? I'm sure you were *young* once."

"Of course."

"Being young *and* a vampire…it's like being young on steroids."

"Yes. It is."

"Of that group downstairs that you murdered…I was the oldest."

Ramonne remained quiet for a moment.

"Suppose…suppose I let you go. Where would you go?"

"Where would you want me to go?"

"Out of Thailand. Back to Russia."

"All right…that's what I'll do."

"No you won't."

Ramonne took the short sword and drew it swiftly across Goran's throat. Immediately blood began spraying. Ramonne held Goran by his long blond hair and sawed his head off.

16

Laem Singh Temple was just a few blocks from the 9th Floor
building but because of Patong's configuration of one-way
streets, it took close to an hour for the little caravan to negotiate
the crowded streets. Patong is most active between the hours of
midnight and 3:00 a.m. It was just after 1:00 a.m. when they
arrived at the temple gate.

The gate was open and the Hummer and the RV passed
through unopposed. The interior of each vehicle contained rolls
of plastic sheets, which held a thoroughly disgusting array of
human—and non-human—remains.

As Ramonne had predicted, Narong's men, including
Krung, had not been killed by the monsters that attacked them,
and they were able to help with the clean-up. However, when
the corpses were tossed into the two waste bins and the heads
stowed in garbage bags, Ramonne put the four under his spell.
He then—swiftly—drained the rest of their lifeblood.

Nanork tried to stop this, but Ramonne reacted violently
and held him at bay with one strong arm while he completed
his grisly task. He then explained that if he had not killed them,
they would have been turned into vampires. He spared them

the indignity of having their heads removed, and tossed their corpses into the RV.

The two huge waste bins were rolled into the street—awaiting their nightly pick-up.

At the temple, Ramonne directed the professor to drive the RV to a large parking lot facing a small temple with a chimney and a dozen steps ascending to its entrance.

A half-dozen monks started across the parking lot, but before they reached the group, they were already under Ramonne's spell. Without any words exchanged, the monks began loading tinder and logs into the crematorium. When it was ready, they lit the tinder and watched as the fire started and the interior chamber began to glow. One of them nodded to Ramonne, and he instructed Nanork to start to empty the plastic-wrapped contents of the two vehicles into the two plain wooden coffins the monks provided.

Nanork and the monks carried the coffins and inserted them one at a time into the crematorium.

The entire process from the clean-up of the restaurant to the cremation of the remains was watched silently by Juliette. Rather than being repulsed, she was fascinated. When the second coffin slid into the crematorium, Ramonne nodded to the professor, who handed a large wad of cash to the eldest monk. The monks bowed profusely as the small entourage got in their vehicles and departed.

————

It was a few hours before dawn when the group crossed the bridge to the mainland and were on the highway headed to the east coast.

The professor was at the wheel of the RV, and Ramonne and Juliette were reclining on the bed in the rear.

"What was all that about, my love?" Juliette asked coquettishly.

"You've heard of gangsters referring to a *cleaner?*"

"Someone who comes in and cleans up the mess."

"Exactly. That's what I was hired to do. Clean up a mess."

"Seems to me you made a very big mess. *Un grand désordre.* We cut off their heads. You cremated their heads. They weren't human."

"No. They were like me."

"No, my love. They were not like you. They were pigs." She shifted onto her elbows and stared into his eyes. "Tell me."

"All right. In order to be rid of Goran and the others, you have to expose them to sunlight, or cut off their heads and incinerate them on sacred ground."

"You left two garbage bins with a half-dozen headless corpses. Won't that be suspicious?"

"No. Thailand is not terribly careful in the disposal of its trash. An old truck will arrive just before dawn and the whole bin will be dumped into the back by an automated arm, and it will be disposed of in a huge incinerator, without ever having been examined by a human being."

"Fascinating."

"Boring. You're much more fascinating."

Before he knew what was happening, the professor felt the rear of the RV start to move up and down and side to side.

He held the wheel firmly and silently cursed.

———

The hours from dawn to dusk went by unheeded as the caravan moved first to the east and then, reaching the coast, to the north.

The driver of the Mercedes van was used to the vampire merely appearing alongside him as darkness fell and he emerged from his coffin.

"Where are we?"

"Chumphon, sir."

Ramonne processed this. Chumphon was an unspoiled beachside town on the uncluttered east coast.

"I've heard of this place. I want to stop."

The Mercedes was in the lead, so when the driver pulled over, the others followed suit.

Ramonne got out and went to the RV. He opened the door and extended a hand to Juliette. She stepped out onto the white sand. The horizon glowed with the rising moon. Cliffs and caves were carved into the limestone rock walls that lined the bay before them.

"I propose that you and I spend a few nights here."

Juliette cocked her head and gave him a queer smile.

"Oh? Why is that?"

"We should get to know each other better before we return to the madness of Krung Thep."

"Krung Thep?"

"Bangkok."

Juliette studied Ramonne's handsome face...She learned nothing.

"Who goes? Who stays?"

"Well, I don't drive, so the professor stays."

"And?"

"And...I sleep in a coffin, so the van stays with its driver. The Humvee with Nanork goes back to Bangkok."

She pouted. "Do you really have to sleep in a coffin?"

He hesitated. "No, not really. But I prefer it."

"You *prefer* it. Just like a *man*."

"I am not a *man*. I am much, *much* more."

"Oh, of course you are...All right. The van stays. With its driver. But why does the professor stay?"

"Where will you sleep?" Ramonne asked.

"In a hotel, silly."

That evening, the professor in the RV, and Nanork in the Humvee returned to Bangkok, while Ramonne and Juliette checked into the Magic House on Coral Beach. The van driver felt safest staying with the vehicle, knowing the price he would pay should anything happen to his charge.

———

"So what happened after Jim Thompson disappeared?"

"I felt terrible. I couldn't find him. It wasn't until years later that I put it together. The Black Dragons tracked him to Malaysia and killed him."

"I'm sorry."

Ramonne and Juliette were in a seafood shack on a newly-built pier on the crescent-shaped Coral Beach. Juliette shucked fresh clams and dipped them in garlic and butter, while Ramonne sipped his own La Piuma Montepulciano. He'd found the Italian wine available in the better markets of Bangkok, and very drinkable. So rather than raid his cellar, he sent the professor to procure a half-dozen bottles for the trip.

"He was a good, very dear friend."

"I'm sure he was." Juliette's attention was on two foreign men who had just entered the bar. They were well into their sixties. They had a boy with them. The boy was Thai or Burmese. About twelve or fourteen.

Ramonne followed her glare. Instantly he *saw* what she saw. They were abusing the boy. Physically. Sexually.

Ramonne got up. He approached them.

"Good evening, gentlemen."

They gave him an odd look and tried to ignore him.

"Might I ask your relationship with this young lad?"

"The oldest of the two scowled at him. "None of your business. Fuck off."

Ramonne leaned a little closer. "I'll ask you again. I suggest you give your answer some serious thought."

"He's our son. Now, as I said before…*kindly* fuck off."

Ramonne looked the terrified boy in his eyes. What he saw told him everything he needed to know. He reached out and snapped the neck of the first German. The second was in shock and getting to his feet to run, when Ramonne—literally—broke him in half.

Ramonne quickly put the boy into a trance and dragged the corpses onto the pier. He took a chance and drained the blood from one before tossing them over the railing.

He apologized to Juliette. "Sorry...I needed that."

She pulled him close and kissed him. She could taste the German's blood, and smiled when she released him.

Ramonne knew their corpses would reappear, and even if no one else remembered what happened, floating corpses were always trouble.

They had to leave.

———

So instead of a romantic tryst on the beach, Juliette found herself accompanying a twelve-year-old Burmese boy to Bangkok, while her erstwhile lover slept behind a curtain in his coffin.

The boy, named Arun, had been travelling with the Germans for two weeks. He came from Yangon, the largest city in Myanmar, or Burma. He was basically ignored by his family. He had two sisters that his parents were trying to find husbands for. He had attended the first "Pride" festival this year in the city parks, without knowing what any of the overtly gay pageantry meant.

He was approached by the Germans and succumbed to the first real human kindness he had ever experienced. His parents had merely tolerated him for twelve years. But this felt different. They bought him sweets, ice cream—his first. The festival had a carnival, and they took him on rides. At night they brought him to his home. His father welcomed them. He introduced his sisters to them. They had brought sugar-cane whiskey. They stayed late—and ignored the girls. The boy was sleepy but he heard talk about a meeting the next day.

The following day, the father forbade the boy from going back to the festival. Instead he told him to pack a bag. He would be taking a trip with the *ninenkasar*—the foreigners.

That afternoon, a village elder arrived, and his father signed a number of documents. When finished, the man handed his father a passport.

In the beginning, it was fun. They played games. Innocent games. The Germans had a crew cab pickup truck with a cover over the back—called a "Carryboy" in Thailand and Mynamar. They'd take turns sleeping in the back. Under the cover. But soon, Arun found he was not alone.

And it went on from there.

After four or five days, Arun wanted to go home, but Gunther—the older of the two—told him he was now their "son."

He would be living with them from now on.

Juliette held him until he fell asleep on her breast.

17

May

Martin and Ben rode together in Martin's BMW. They were silent the entire time from when Ben was picked up until they arrived at the Supreme Court building

Each was lost in their own thoughts on this, the final day of their appeal in the lower court ruling that cleared Sarawat Construction, and specifically its owner Vithiya Sarawat, from any and all charges filed by Martin in the death of his son and three others.

Martin had convinced Ben to use his Thai legal team to persuade the families of the three others that he would personally assure them that they would be compensated fairly—if there could ever be such a price—for their loss, whether they lost or won, and so they formed a class action suit against Sarawat Construction. The two who were wounded had accepted the payment offered as settlement.

On this day, Ben had been granted the extreme privilege of presenting and questioning their only eyewitness to the accident.

The building was a magnificent blend of Siamese and

European design that reflected the grand era of late-nineteenth century architecture in Bangkok. Compared to the drab gray buildings that Martin and Ben had become used to in pursuit of justice, this three-storied marvel encompassed the entire block.

Ben showed their IDs at the gate and they were smartly saluted and told to proceed to the parking area.

Ben showed him another document and pointed to the Range Rover that was directly behind them. The guard studied the paper and then went to the other vehicle. After a moment's discussion, both vehicles were allowed to enter.

They parked and Martin told Ben to wait in the car while he went to the Range Rover. He tapped on the driver's glass and the window went down. The professor nodded.

"How is she?"

"See for yourself." The professor leaned back so Martin could see his passenger.

Juliette was asleep.

"Jesus. Wake her up."

"Not that easy. You want her awake or you want her lucid?"

"For Christ's sake. She's our witness. Our *only* witness. We need her able to fucking talk."

"All right." The professor opened a little leather bag. He withdrew a syringe and a small vial. He filled the syringe, tapped the needle to release several drops, and then swiftly injected Juliette.

The reaction was instantaneous.

She bolted upright. She looked sideways at the professor. She smiled.

"Good morning, *mon chérie*."

The professor nodded and moved back so she could see Martin.

"Juliette. Do you know where you are?"

She ran her fingers through her hair and opened her purse. She took out a small mirror and a lipstick tube. She applied the lipstick and closed the bag.

Ben was now standing alongside the car, and he opened the door for her. She gave him her hand, and he helped her out.

She took Ben's arm and, as they started to walk to the courthouse, she looked back at Martin's astonished face.

"Come on, Martin. We don't want to be late."

———

The tedious courtroom procedure took longer than all the others, as they were now in the upper echelon of Thai pomp and pageantry. The very building spoke of eloquence and ostentation. The only thing missing were powdered wigs, which Martin was surprised they hadn't purloined from the British.

Eventually Juliette was called as a witness.

It had been over an hour since they had entered the courtroom, and Martin was quite surprised to find her as coherent as she was when Ben questioned her.

"You were the last person to see Hon Larue alive, is that correct?"

"I suppose I was."

"Can you tell me why you and he were crossing Soi Langsuan at 10:40 p.m. on December 24th."

"To get to the other side?"

Ben stared blankly at her.

"That's a joke."

"Please. Tell us what happened."

"Hon and I, we had a fight at Mr. Martin's Christmas party, and we left. The fight got worse as we descended to the street and I—"

A Thai lawyer for the other side raised a question. Once it was translated, it meant that they didn't understand why she *descended* to the street. Ben explained that Martin lived on the sixteenth floor of his apartment building—something that had been recorded into the trial transcripts numerous times.

The judge allowed Ben to resume his questioning of his

witness.

"I went out into the street—not paying any attention to the traffic. I got lucky and crossed safely to the other side."

"And Hon?"

Juliette looked down at her lap for a moment, and then she looked back up and focused on the judge.

"He followed me…but he wasn't so lucky."

Ben spoke quietly.

"What happened?"

"The sky opened. The heavens exploded and dumped asteroids and space particles in great, great abundance. It smothered him…it crushed him."

She looked at Ben. "The heavens descended upon him and destroyed him."

It was obvious to Martin that now she was in a trance.

Not knowing what to ask, Ben said, "Do you know why this happened?"

"I have no fucking idea."

The judge looked at Ben. He banged his gavel.

"We will take a short recess. Both parties will meet me in chambers."

———

Martin took Juliette out of the courtroom and sat with her on a bench in the hallway.

She had a sideways smile that revealed absolutely nothing about the chaos she had just caused.

It was less than a half-hour when Ben emerged.

All Martin had to see was his face to know the outcome.

"We lost. Didn't we?"

Ben swallowed and sat next to Juliette. "Yes. We lost."

Martin hung his head.

Ben put a hand on his shoulder. "We did nothing wrong, Martin."

Martin looked at Juliette. His eyes furrowed.

"It wasn't her. We knew she was a risk. She told them what she saw. It made no difference. We were on the wrong side from the beginning."

Martin clenched his fist. "File another appeal."

"Martin...That would take years."

"I don't care."

Ben put his hand over his fist. "I know you. You think you can right any wrong. You think if you are right, you can win...Well, as your attorney, and your friend, I'm here to tell you...you can't. Sometimes you lose.

"We just lost. Now you have to get on with your life."

———

The Friday afternoon traffic was horrendous. Normally Martin would have joined Ben when he jumped out of the car and headed for the skytrain. But Martin didn't care. He was lost in his thoughts, and time meant nothing to him. It was an hour after dusk when Martin arrived home.

Areeya greeted him at the door. He had called her from the car, so she already knew they had lost their appeal. She pulled him to her and held him until he was able to look at her without tears in his eyes.

"We lost."

"No. You didn't lose. You fought for justice. You fought for our son. You fought the good fight."

She held him at arm's length and looked into his bloodshot eyes. "Look what you did for the families of the workers that were killed. You've already changed their lives. Their loss was not in vain because of you."

"But ours was. No matter how hard we tried—"

"No. Do *not* trivialize our loss. We watched our son's body burn in a furnace. We have his ashes in an urn. I don't want his ashes. I want him."

Now it was Martin's turn to hold her. He pulled her to him and kissed the top of her head as she quietly sobbed.

He felt her regaining strength, and he looked down at her and smiled.

"I have an idea. A way to make us feel better."

"Yes?"

"We start a school and an orphanage here in Bangkok—for the children of Burmese workers."

Her hands dropped down to his side and she took hold of his right one. She smiled.

"Funny you should say that. Your 'professor' friend stopped by a little while ago with a note…and a package."

Martin was definitely curious. "Yes?"

"The package is in the den. Come with me."

Wiping the last tears from her eyes, she smiled broadly as she walked with Martin to the den.

Seated in a large rattan wingback chair, completely entranced with the city skyline before him, was Arun.

"Who is *he*?"

"His name is Arun. Read the letter."

Martin opened the envelope. In old-fashioned, elegant cursive handwriting it read:

Martin,

Nothing can replace your loss. But here is a lost soul who needs you. Needs your guidance. Needs a home. His own family, I'm afraid, gave him away for a few coins, and he should definitely not be returned to them. He's been abused, so he will need time to heal.

It was signed simply, "R."

The boy turned from the window and looked at Martin. He instinctively reached out to Areeya, who took his hand.

Martin smiled and slowly introduced himself in Burmese. The boy was amazed to hear a foreigner speak his language. He relaxed a little and exchanged bows with Martin.

Martin asked his age and where he was from. The boy was polite but guarded, and offered no more than exactly what he was asked.

Just then, Soon arrived with little Nina. Nina was in a school play and had just returned from rehearsal. She hugged her mom and dad and then crossed her arms and stared at Arun.

"Who is this?"

"His name is Arun. He's Burmese," Areeya replied.

"Obviously. What's he doing here?"

Areeya started to attempt to explain, but Martin put a hand on her knee and took over. "He's on his own. He needs a home."

"Where are his parents?"

"In Myanmar. But they were not good parents. They sold him to bad people."

"They *sold* him?" Slowly Nina uncrossed her arms and her frown turned to curiosity tinged with anger.

"Yes, honey. That's why we're going to give him a new home. In fact, we're going to give many children of Burmese workers a school in Bangkok, and for those that need it—like Arun—a home."

The boy watched in wonder as this scene played out in English—a language he had virtually no knowledge of. In the past 48 hours the bad men he had come to hate had mysteriously disappeared, and he found himself with a kind and very pretty white lady who traveled in a large, futuristic van that was sometimes occupied by a mysterious but oddly trustworthy white man. They travelled back to Krung Thep, where he and the disgusting European men had been before. Here he was given a fine room of his own, and all he wanted to eat. Clothing was bought for him, and shortly he was brought to this magnificent home, high in the skies, where he was watching the strange play unfolding before him.

He'd been fed once since he'd arrived, and he figured if he just stayed quiet, he might get fed again.

18

___

The boy slept in the guest room. All of Nina's many questions had been answered. In doing so, Martin now had a plan—one that excited him and Areeya. Instead of going to bed feeling exhausted and defeated, they had a sense of something new and positive coming into their life.

They made love. They seemed to have their life back. They fell asleep in each other's arms.

___

Martin slept soundly for the first time in what seemed like months. He even dreamed. In his dream he showered and got dressed. He put on a tuxedo, an affectation he rarely succumbed to. He groomed himself and headed for the lobby.

A black Mercedes awaited him, and the driver held the door for him. He rode silently through the darkened city. There were no thoughts of his family or any of the events of the past several weeks. In the dream, he was free of any and all restraints, and on his way to an adventure. The cityscape was full of wonder to him as it passed by his window.

Eventually the car stopped and the driver opened his door.

He entered a massive chrome and marble lobby.

A uniformed guard pressed the button for the penthouse. The *only* button.

He had been asleep until now. He awoke with a start as his eyes focused on the sparkling city skyline as the cab continued to climb. He gasped as he tried to catch his breath.

Finally the cab slowed to a stop. The door opened and, to Martin's utter amazement, he saw Vithiya Sarawat standing in front of a two-story window, also wearing a tuxedo, and holding a champagne flute. The man's face had been burned into his psyche as a black-and-white image appearing occasionally in the newspaper. But this was the first time he'd seen him in the flesh.

Next to Vithiya was a gorgeous Asian woman in a sleek black dress, and a nattily attired Ramonne Delacroix with Juliette. She was as elegantly dressed as the other woman, and she smiled warmly at Martin.

There were about two dozen other guests. Mainly couples. All fashionably dressed—the men in tuxedos and the women in lavish satin, taffeta, or silk gowns. The gorgeous jewelry on display sparkled each time the ladies moved.

Vithiya turned as the elevator door closed. "Who the hell is this?"

Ramonne picked up a champagne glass as he walked towards Martin. "This…" He handed the champagne to Martin. "This is Martin Larue. He is my guest." Ramonne put his arm around Martin's shoulder and walked him into the room.

"How did he get past the guards?"

"I took care of that." Ramonne smiled.

Vithiya was confused.

"Come now. You have *me*. You don't need your guards. I thought we were here to celebrate?"

Vithiya gave Martin another look and then raised his glass to Ramonne. "You took care of a problem for me. Cleanly. Efficiently. I am forever indebted to you."

Ramonne raised his glass in a toast. "You hired me to do a job. I did it. Let's keep it simple." He downed his champagne. "Come. Let's go out on the roof. It's a beautiful night."

The penthouse reception had direct access onto the roof that served as the helicopter pad for Vithiya's personal Sikorsky helicopter. Two guards were stationed at the heavy padded doors, but they opened them when given a nod by Vithiya.

A cool breeze blew in contrast to the stifling heat on the ground sixty floors below. The full moon seemed within arm's reach. The helicopter was absent, and the large space was akin to being on the top of a mountain—with a teeming city below instead of a natural landscape.

"Seriously. How do I repay you?"

Ramonne smiled. "What do you have in mind?"

"Work for me."

"Work for *you*…? I work for Ping."

"I'll pay you double."

Ramonne laughed. "That's exactly what Ping said to me tonight."

Vithiya didn't laugh. "What were you talking about?"

"Killing you, of course."

Vithiya looked nervously about. Besides the guests, there were a half-dozen armed guards.

And there was the man who came up in the elevator alone.

"Tell me again who he is?"

"I told you…Martin Larue."

"Why is he here?"

Ramonne smiled. "Justice."

"*Justice?*"

"Yes. He was denied it."

Suddenly Vithiya had an epiphany. "I know who he is. He challenged us in court."

"And he didn't get justice."

"He lost."

"No. He was denied justice."

Vithiya laughed. "This is Thailand. Justice is for sale. It depends on how rich you are. Unfortunately, I'm richer."

Ramonne grabbed Vithiya by his collar and dragged him over to Martin. Two guards started to move, but Ramonne merely put up a hand and they stopped.

"I offer you justice." Ramonne held Vithiya so he was pinned against the safety rail that ran around the helicopter pad perimeter.

Vithiya began to get worried. "What are you doing?"

Martin shook his head. He didn't have to speak the words for Ramonne to hear him. *'I can't.'*

Ramonne lifted Vithiya and stared into Martin's eyes. *'Of course you can. Just say the word.'*

Martin spoke. "All I wanted was an admission of guilt."

Ramonne looked at Vithiya. "You hear that? All he wants is an admission of guilt. You can do *that*, can't you?" He held him so half his body was dangling over the sixty-story building.

Vithiya gripped Ramonne's arm in abject terror.

"I...I admit it. I'm responsible. I allowed my contractors to break the laws to save money."

Martin was aghast. "You *allowed* them?"

"All right. I *told* them to do it."

Ramonne continued to dangle Vithiya over the edge while he waited for Martin's response.

Finally, Martin nodded. "Let him go."

Vithiya looked relieved. However, Ramonne had not brought him back onto the deck. He was still precariously held over the edge.

"Please."

"We haven't settled your payment to me."

"What do you want? Name anything."

Ramonne smiled. "What do I want...? I want you to *die*."

He released his grip and Vithiya fell eight hundred feet to the street below.

———

In those bizarre moments after Vithiya went off the building, Martin was frozen in shock.

"What did you do?"

"What needed to be done."

"But...I'll be blamed for this."

"No one saw anything. Look around."

It was true. There wasn't anyone paying attention to them. Not even the guards.

However, down below could be heard the shrieking of sirens.

"I have to go." Ramonne vaulted easily onto the parapet. He turned back, and he and Martin locked eyes.

Ramonne spoke: "It had to be done."

Neither knew if or when they would see each other again.

"Thank you."

Without replying, Ramonne leapt and landed on a construction crane twenty stories below. He looked back up at the Sarawat Communications name in neon on the side of the helipad, and the lone figure standing above it.

———

Martin wasn't sure how long he had stared into the night with the image of Vithiya falling off the building burned into his memory. It was a voice gently speaking his name that brought him out of the trance.

"Khun Martin...Mr. Larue?"

Martin turned and was surprised to see Sergeant Prasert Theeravit. He was not alone. A half-dozen brown uniformed police were questioning the guests of the party.

"Sergeant Prasert."

"Mr. Larue. What can you tell me about Khun Vithiya's death."

"I don't know what you're talking about…Vithiya Sarawat is *dead*?"

"Yes. He fell, jumped, or was pushed from this building."

"That's terrible. I was just talking to him not twenty minutes ago."

"After you talked with him, where did he go?"

"He talked to some other guests. It was his party and he was making the rounds."

Sergeant Prasert made a few notes and then closed his notebook. He had a puzzled look. "Mr. Larue. Why were you here tonight? As I understand it, this party was to celebrate Khun Vithiya's win in court today. A case, I believe, that you were involved in."

Martin took a minute before answering. "I indeed was involved in the case in court today. It was an appeal of a lawsuit in the death of my son on Christmas Eve…You remember that night, don't you?"

"Of course."

"We lost our appeal and Khun Vithiya won. My appearance here tonight was, as they say, to extend an olive branch. To show that there is to be no further friction between us."

Sergeant Prasert said nothing but just stared at Martin.

Finally, Martin set his empty glass down. "If there's nothing else, sergeant, I'd like to go now."

Sergeant Prasert continued to stare for a few more moments and then he stepped aside. "Of course."

He motioned to one of his officers. "Please see that Mr. Larue is escorted to his home.

19

Studio 8 at Moonstar Studios was set up as a concert hall. Risers had been assembled in a semi-circle and several hundred comfortable chairs had been installed. On the raised stage, a guitar, a stand-up bass, and a drum kit flanked a massive Yamaha Disklavier grand piano. Three movie screens were hung against the dark-blue curtain.

The room was full. In the center of the audience sat Martin, Areeya, and Nina. The lights dimmed and an image was projected on the center screen. It was a beautiful photo of a single lotus blossom—the cover of the album *Yang Yu* by Hon Larue. The audience applauded. Areeya squeezed Martin's hand. John, Ben, and Nippy came on stage and settled behind their instruments.

Next to appear was Simon, the record company attorney who had become Hon's manager and the album's producer.

"Good evening. *Sawasdee khrap.*" He bowed politely to the audience. "We are gathered here tonight to celebrate the life of Hon Larue, and the premiere performance of his album *Yang Yu*. For those who don't know, *yang yu* means 'still here.' It was Hon's prophetic title for the album, from the beginning.

"I met Hon just two years ago when he was performing at

Vienna's Konzerthaus with Yo-Yo Ma. I had never heard a performance like it, and was stunned to learn that he was just sixteen. Our journey together took us around the globe and finally back to his home in Bangkok, where he wanted to rehearse and start recording his first and, unfortunately, *only* album. However, I am pleased to say that there are enough live recordings of his various concerts, that I will be busy for several years to come archiving and producing successive works, so that his legacy will truly live on.

"Hon's life was an incredible journey. From an orphanage in Cambodia to the concert halls of Europe, he was beloved by all who knew him. He had a magical way of making people feel at ease the moment they met him. Blessed with enormous talent, he had virtually no ego, and was one of the shiest people I've ever known. He didn't care about fame, he just wanted to create. To write his gorgeous music and play it for the world.

"Tonight we will hear *Yang Yu* as it will be released. Hon's cohorts are here with us. On guitar, John Sterling...Ben Howard on bass...And Nippy Noya on drums. And playing Hon's magnificent piano compositions, just as he recorded them, will be this beautiful Yamaha Disklavier. For those of you who are not familiar with the instrument, it will faithfully reproduce every nuance of Hon's performance, as if he were here performing it for you himself.

"And now, please enjoy *Yang Yu*."

The audience applauded politely as the lights dimmed and single spots highlighted the three musicians. The light on the piano was broader and tinted blue. The bass player started a slow lament as the album cover graphics appeared on the center screen. The guitar came in with some very sparse, hollow notes, and finally the drums laid down a very soft beat on brushes. It was several minutes before the first piano sounds were heard—and these were chords...moving progressively up and down until they finally settled and a melody was begun with the right hand.

The sound was truly amazing. Martin—who had probably heard his son play the piano more than anyone else in the room—reckoned there was no difference in what he was hearing tonight than when he listened to this same piece in rehearsal a few months before. He had Areeya on one side and Nina on the other, and both were squeezing his hands with all their emotional might. Tears welled up in their eyes, and in the eyes of most of the family and friends gathered. The imagery on the stage changed slowly...photos of Hon in his youth, dissolving into performance studies of him enraptured in his art.

Martin looked about the room. Everyone important to him was there. The group from Christmas Eve sat together just in front of Martin. Areeya's large family was present. Many of Hon's college classmates were scattered throughout the theater.

In the very last row, Martin was glad to see his truly *oldest* friend. He was seated next to *her*, but Martin bore her no grudge. He had come to understand her problems and accept them.

Martin smiled and turned back to the stage. His wife put her head on his shoulder and his daughter released her grip on his arm.

Without music, life would be a mistake. He wondered where he'd heard this?

EPILOGUE

Provence, France

The moon was slowly rising over a Van Gogh sky. Another Mercedes Sprinter van was parked alongside a billowing field. Other than the sky, the marsh, and the van, there appeared to be nothing else on Earth.

A *whoosh* and the side door of the van opened. Juliette smiled and extended her hand to Ramonne. He stepped into the beauty of the night.

"*C'est magnifique.*"

They were in the Camargue regional park and nature reserve —a protected area about 100 kilometers northwest of Marseilles.

This was nearly the end of a very long journey. Three nights ago, they'd flown from Bangkok to Paris. This was on a private plane that allowed them enough time to depart an hour after sunset and reach their hotel in Saint-Germain before the sun rose. The professor was with them on that flight, but he'd stayed at the airport and traveled on to Marseilles to complete the arrangements for the rest of their journey.

Juliette and Ramonne slept the next day and then arose to

wander the streets while Juliette regaled Ramonne with her "former" life in the eighteenth century. Ramonne was completely enraptured by her tales of depravity. She took him to the Place de l'Hôtel-de-Ville, a charming park in front of the City Hall. A roller-skating rink was set up on this day, being enjoyed by many youngsters.

However, from the thirteenth to the seventeenth century, it was no pleasant park. Under the Old Regime, it was where crowds gathered to witness justice being dispensed in its cruelest forms. Criminals could be executed by hanging, decapitation, burning alive, boiling alive, being broken on a wheel, or by drawing and quartering.

In October 1789, Dr. Joseph-Ignace Guillotin, in the interest of finding a more humane method, successfully had the means of execution changed to decapitation by a machine he perfected—the guillotine. Juliette proudly showed him the location of the first beheading on the Place du Carrousel, next to the Tuileries Palace.

The Revolution blossomed, and on the 21st of January 1793, King Louis XVI was executed on the Place de la Concorde, renamed the Place de la Révolution.

As she told all of this, of course, Ramonne witnessed it firsthand—as if he were actually present as it occurred.

And as his bloodlust adventures had enraptured Juliette, so her crimson-soaked reminiscences engorged him, and they lusted for each other the moment they retreated to their bed sheets.

They allowed themselves three nights of frolicking in Paris before taking a night train to Marseilles, where the professor met them at Arles with a brand-new customized Sprinter van. Ramonne was puzzled that the steering wheel was on the left, but gave it very little thought, glad as he was to see his formidable coffin safely ensconced in a vehicle on French soil. He climbed in and told Juliette to join him. She declined. "Rest, my darling. We have a short trip ahead of us, but there are places where we must stop."

The first stop was the Camargue. The field was surrounded by wetlands. In the distance stood the Luberon Mountains. It was a magnificent spot, and Ramonne drank it in.

Juliette raised a hand, motioning for him to be silent. Then she put her fingers in each side of her mouth and emitted a loud shrill whistle.

Ramonne looked at her in anticipation. She whistled again.

A thunderous noise began to echo over a valley in the distance. Ramonne saw a cloud of dust moving in their direction. Then the water at the far side of the marsh began to splash, and suddenly a herd of small horses charged through the brush towards them. Predominately white in color with small patches of brown and auburn, these gorgeous animals encircled them.

Ramonne marveled at it all. The horses were miniature. Under 150 centimeters. He towered over them.

Ignoring Ramonne, the horses were completely under Juliette's spell. They lined up to nuzzle her.

"I take it you know these horses?"

"I'm not sure if I know *these* horses. I've been coming here for a very long time. But *they* know me."

———

They spent close to an hour with the magnificent beasts. Juliette climbed on one and encouraged Ramonne to do the same. He politely declined but was suitably impressed at her skill as she galloped through the marshes bareback.

Back in the van, Juliette relaxed in a comfortable seat as Ramonne sat on the edge of his coffin.

"Those horses are among the oldest in the world. And probably the toughest. The ancient *gardians* or 'cowboys'—pardon me for using such a vulgar term—tend them here in the marshes while moving their herds of black bulls. They also prize them as their choice of steed for the bull fights."

"Of course. The *corrida*. My father took me to the arena in Arles when I was a boy. It saddened me to see the bull killed in the end."

"Really? That was my favorite part…Unless of course the *torero* was gored."

Ramonne looked at her. He thought to himself, *What an odd creature.*

"How much farther are we going?" he asked

Juliette looked out the window. "About another hour."

"Good. Then there's time for you to tell me."

"Tell you…? Tell you what?"

"Who you are."

"*Who I am*? You know who I am."

"No. How is it possible that you are…so *old.*"

"Really? Am I too old for you?" she flirted with him.

"You know what I mean. I know why I am still alive. I'm a vampire. But what are you?"

"You're not *alive*. You *exist*. As do I."

The Sprinter had comfortable reclining leather seats just behind the driver's compartment. A bar was mounted in the panel that separated them from the driver. A table fit snugly up against the front of the coffin behind them. Both the chairs could be converted into a comfortable bed if desired. At the moment they were seated, sipping a fine Châteauneuf-du-Pape.

Outside, a full moon bathed a gorgeous landscape of flowing vineyards and orchards.

"Very well…Let me start at the beginning. As a child, my sister Justine and I were raised in a convent. The Pentemont in the Rue de Grenelle in the 7th arrondissement. The prettiest and most immoral girls in Paris were those that came from the Pentemont. The churches served as bordellos."

"I know that building," Ramonne interrupted. "When I was a boy, it was home to the Imperial Guard."

"That was after I left."

"So, you are actually *older* than me?"

"Darling, this story is not about how *old* I am. It's about *who* I am."

"Please. Continue."

"As I said, it was in the convent that I was transformed from an innocent child to a purveyor of wanton debaucheries. At the tender age of thirteen, I was placed in the tutelage of Madame Delbane, who immediately confessed to me that she took great inner pleasure from her conviction that a 'good reputation is a valueless encumbrance.' It can never compensate us for what it costs us in sacrifice."

She drained her glass and Ramonne refilled it. "But…" he objected. "What of the consequences?"

"What consequences?" she retorted. "She taught me to fear I'd taste too many pleasures. She beseeched me to find in crime the same happiness as she, and to strive as time passed to make of evil-doing a habit, until, with the passing of time, I had become so endeared to the habit, that I literally could not go on without imbibing of this potent drink…

"Thus my education began. Within the next few years, I partook of virtually every form of depravity."

The imagery that accompanied this revelation was nothing short of pornographic. Nubile young maidens being divested of their flimsy garments and triggered into orgiastic ecstasy by older nymphomaniac nuns."

For Ramonne, the debauchery was quite clear. "Impressive. But increasingly cruel." He filled his glass.

"Maybe it was the time. This was just prior to *La Revolution*. We were wanton children, impressionable."

"You were how old when you left the convent?"

"Nineteen."

"And how old were you when the Revolution started?"

"Thirty."

"So you are seventy years older than me?"

"You're one hundred and ninety years old. What difference does another seventy make?"

"Absolutely nothing. As they say, age is just a number…So tell me what happened next."

"Well, I met an older girl who had been raped and sodomized, and we left the convent together to seek out vengeance on the male race."

"I see." Literally. "And next?"

"Ah. Next it was Saint-Fond, rich beyond imagination, who enlisted me to commit incest with his daughter, murder his father, and torture young girls to death on a daily basis."

"I take it that was not the end of your journey."

"No. I won't bore you with the rest. You get the picture…Madame Delbane broke the hymen and Monsieur Saint-Fond found the clitoris."

"And the monster was released."

She nestled into his lap. "I became who I am."

"But that was a very long time ago. How have you survived?"

She stared out the window. They were entering the mountain village of Bonnieux.

"That is a question that you will learn the answer to soon enough. But first let's stop and have a brief repast."

She leaned over the partition and told the professor to make a left turn as the road ascended, and to park where he could.

They all disembarked and walked up a cobblestone road flanked by ancient walls. Ramonne knew the village, but it had been so long ago that all he had were a few boyhood memories of his grandmother taking him to the weekly market. They passed the village grocer, and then Juliette led them down a steep path.

On each side, houses seemed to have been carved out of the rock—hundreds of years ago. They reached the bottom—a lovely terrace that looked out over the valley below.

On the left, a *taverne* was also carved into the hillside. Here,

Juliette excused herself and went in to talk with the proprietor. An inviting open-air dining area extended from the inn, overlooking the valley. It was ringed with strings of dim bare bulbs, and held a dozen or so people.

Ramonne led the professor to a comfortable table at the edge, where the nighttime view was spectacular.

"I took the liberty of ordering. A *salade niçoise* and *beouf à la Gardienne* for myself and the doctor. And a couple of bottles of Château Vignelaure."

When she finished describing the order, there was a well-built man in a soiled apron at their table with three glasses and two bottles. He set them all in the middle of the table and retreated. Juliette did the pouring.

She raised her glass. "To the journey's end." They clinked their glasses and downed the wine.

Ramonne surveyed their setting. They were on a plateau that served as a parking lot for an ancient church. A half-dozen weather-worn gargoyles were being repaired and looked like large sleeping dogs.

Turning back to the tavern and its terrace, he studied the customers. There was an elderly couple, each absorbed in a book. Several families with young children or an infant in a stroller. The parents were attempting to enjoy their meal while minding the children. Being France, of course there was a pair of young lovers, entwined in each other's arms and sipping their drinks while stealing kisses as they watched the moon move across the valley.

He smiled with great satisfaction as he realized he had finally returned to a place where life was actually being *lived*. There wasn't a single blue screen in anybody's hand. No one was texting or scrolling or "tweeting" or "zooming" or "pinging."

They were talking, reading, playing with their kids, or falling in love.

Living life.

He felt like he was home at last.

Juliette was watching him. He 'sighed' and she reached out and took his left hand. *"N'est-ce pas merveilleux?"*

He turned to face her. "Yes. It's perfect. But, this is not actually our journey's end, is it?"

"No, *mon chérie*." She pointed across the valley to a small hillside village whose lights twinkled in the distance. *"That* is our destination."

As he turned to look, the same burly waiter arrived with their meals. Ramonne felt slightly nauseous, as he always did, when the scent of freshly cooked meat caught his nostrils, and he excused himself and stood to let them enjoy their repast.

He wandered to the church garden and realized that it was actually a small graveyard. There were no more than a dozen headstones left. But he knew that the village and all around them had been the scene, centuries ago, of terrible religious wars with French Catholics slaughtering French Protestants down to the last living child.

His mind rambled back to his early childhood in Avignon, barely sixty kilometers away, and the fateful day in 1858 when he sailed from Marseilles with the legendary Henri Mouhot to explore *Indochine.*

Juliette gently took his arm. "We're finished."

He looked back to the table. The professor was wiping his lips with a starched napkin.

She pointed again at the distant village. "Do you see the castle at the top of the village?"

"It's half destroyed."

"That's our final destination."

Behind them the church bells somberly intoned the hour of midnight.

———

Within thirty minutes they found themselves traveling below the Pont Julien, a two thousand-year-old Roman bridge. Ramonne silently marveled at the architectural skills of the Romans that allowed them control of their environment two millennia ago.

Soon they came to a large stone arch. It was the entry to a medieval village.

The professor stopped the van. "Master, we cannot fit through the arch."

Juliette pushed a button and the side door of the van whooshed open. "Go to the left. The road is paved and an easy climb to the top. Pull into the castle entry and we'll meet you there." Ramonne and Juliette stepped out.

The professor slowly proceeded up the blacktopped road while Juliette led the way up the cobblestone path.

"Do you know these stones?"

Ramonne smiled. "My feet trod such stones often in my youth. Stones gathered from the surrounding fields and laid without mortar. Worn smooth by over a thousand years of feet and hooves."

Except for a few porch lights and street lamps, there was no sign of life at this time of night. As they continued their upward stroll, Juliette pointed out several charming doorways. Two were *tavernes*, shuttered for the night. Another was the town hall with an elaborate sun dial, and next to it were stone steps leading down to an enormous wine cellar. This intrigued the vampire and amused Juliette.

"The village dates back to the ninth century."

"Yes. I can *feel* it. We are headed for the castle, *oui*?"

"Yes."

"We will stay there?"

"Yes. It's my uncle's."

"We are arriving late. Won't we awaken him?"

She just smiled.

Finally they reached the top of the village.

The wall surrounding the ancient castle had been recently repaired and fortified. Buttresses had been added of an almost pure white stone. The walls soared twenty meters above their heads. Much of the outer wall lay in ruins, as did much of the castle tower above.

"What happened?"

"*La Revolution*…They came after my uncle. And later, when he was gone, they used the walls as stone for the village."

Ramonne stopped. "Your uncle was *here* in the eighteenth century?"

Juliette smiled. "Yes, *darling*. So was I. Come. He'll explain."

She led them around what would be described as the moat. It was dry, but its steep banks would have prevented an easy assault.

At the far north, the stone path of the village met the blacktop of the modern road. Here the professor was parked. Ramonne and Juliette emerged. Fortunately, the moon had ascended and provided sufficient light to take in the vast exterior entry to the castle. There were no lights and, for all intents and purposes, it was abandoned.

The professor stepped forward. "Master, I have been here a short while and have seen no sign of activity."

Above them were the gatehouses. One on each side of a large iron gate. In medieval times the walls adjoining the gatehouse would be used to send cascades of boiling oil onto any attackers. Considering the complete and utter silence, Ramonne doubted that would be the case tonight.

He tested the bars. They were sturdy and locked in place.

He looked to Juliette. She smiled and produced a small remote control from her skirt pocket. With a click, the gates swung inward, creaking and groaning on their ancient hinges.

"*Voila*."

Ramonne motioned to the professor to follow them as they headed on the bridge over the moat for the castle keep. This was the great tower that was seen from Bonnieux and several other distant vantage points. It was the master's domicile. It's central nervous system.

It was also the part of the castle that had suffered the most visible damage.

At the castle's entrance they encountered a second security gate. Ramonne looked at Juliette. "I assume you have another of your electronic devices for this?"

"No, silly." She smiled. She reached on her tiptoes and pulled a large bronze key off the top of the door frame. With a creak the gate swung open. The massive wooden door was opened with the same key.

The vampire stood in the open doorway and just stared.

Before him was an eleventh-century French castle interior. Vaulted ceilings and truncated columns supported the vast open spaces. Stone stairs rose and fell from each end of the long room they had entered. Juliette did something, and muted light illuminated and accentuated every feature of the dramatic interior.

The rooms were open to the entry, and Ramonne wandered slowly amongst them. Furnishings were combined from multiple periods. A Louis XV dressing table served as a desk; a Louis XVI dining table was surrounded by sturdy Régence chairs. The Sun King's opulence was evident in the mirrors, chandeliers, and candelabras that hung in each room.

The paintings that adorned the bare stone walls were either mythological extravaganzas by the French Old Master Noël Coypel, or rare Caravaggios. There were also several extremely rare Boucher sketches of Louis XV's mistress, as well as a few Hogarth renderings of female models.

All were exceedingly ribald in nature.

"*Bonsoir.*" The word was spoken in such a *sotto voce* that Ramonne wasn't sure he actually heard. He turned and there was a rather gaunt ageless man standing at the far stairway. His hair, neither blond nor gray, was spiky, and he bore an odd resemblance to Sting of the pop band The Police.

Ramonne stared, while his brain flooded with images. He was completely overwhelmed, so Juliette took him by the hand and helped him cross the room to their host.

"*Oncle, c'est* Ramonne Delacroix."

The gaunt man smiled. The lines that accentuated his face formed into a smile. "*Oui*…I know."

Juliette turned to Ramonne. "*Mon chérie, c'est mon oncle.*"

"I know who he is. The Marquis de Sade…I am honored."

——————

It was an hour later and a grand tour had been conducted of the castle keep. The Sprinter van was securely parked in the livery, the professor had been fed and shown to quarters next to the van, and copious amounts of Provençal wine had been consumed.

There was less than an hour of darkness left, and Ramonne figured if he didn't ask now, he might never know.

"Monsieur, how does it happen that you, who perished in 1814, happen to be here in your ancient domicile some two centuries later?"

The Marquis smiled at him, but remained silent. It was the first time he noticed a gold tooth in his lower palate. "I find it a bit disconcerting that you, who are nearly two hundred years old, dare question my ability to be barely a hundred years older than you."

Ramonne drained his glass. "I've tried to have this conversation with your niece, but to no avail. So, *please*, enlighten me."

The marquis stood and walked deliberately to Juliette. He pulled her hair back and then kissed her—forcefully, wantonly. Ramonne started to rise but thought better of it and stayed in his chair.

When he was finished, the marquis let go of Juliette's hair and she stayed prone for several moments as he returned to his chair. When she lifted her head, she smiled at the marquis.

A servant dressed all in black that had hardly been noticed, refilled all their glasses and disappeared.

The marquis wiped his lips with a starched napkin and then spoke directly to Ramonne. "There is a force in this world known as 'Ultimate Evil.' It is absolute and self-sufficient. It is beyond reason or negotiation. Sustained campaigns of organized plunder and violence such as you have no doubt heard about from my niece…they serve as qualification for admittance to this exclusive club."

"You and Juliette are eternal?"

"No. We are *Revenants*. We are *very* hard to kill."

————

Ramonne lay in his coffin in the back of the van and thought about where he was and what he was doing. He had traveled almost ten thousand kilometers, from Bangkok to Provence, taking the professor with him.

He thought he might have a chance at a bit of romance in his life with an admittedly bizarre woman…But at least she was French—*so how bad could it get*?

Apparently very bad—since her "uncle" was the Marquis de Sade.

Finis.

AUTHOR'S NOTE

This one took longer than most. I started it in December 2018 and finished the first draft in July 2020. It was written in my usual manner—in longhand, in cafés and taverns, with my noise-cancelling mini-headphones on.

In Phuket I owe many thanks to Jane Chumkaew and her beautiful Lillo Island restaurant on the soft sands of Kamala Beach, for allowing me to take up valuable space for hours on end.

In Provence, France, the charming Madame Harang provides the perfect writer's sanctuary in her sprawling home nestled in the foothills of the Luberon. Last year, it was Madame who suggested that the Marquis de Sade (whose castle is visible from my favorite table and chair in her garden) was not actually dead—but haunting the area. (Much to the amusement, no doubt, of noted fashion designer Pierre Cardin, who bought the castle and most of the medieval town in 2011.)

Several dear influential friends have passed on since the writing of the last book, and they need to be remembered. The great writer Jerry Hopkins, who encouraged me to write and regaled me with his stories of the Hawaii we both love. Tim Young, who we never thought would die (twice he had a heart attack and walked out of Patpong to Silom, where he flagged down a *tuk tuk* to BNH Hospital). And Brad Kenny of the Rotary Club Patong Beach, who asked me to write a Vampire of Siam tale set in Phuket. Rest in peace all. You are all sorely missed.

Writing requires discipline—something I normally lack. It is a 'wake up call' for your brain. And it's a wonderfully 'solitary' sport. But when the work is done, it takes a team to turn it into a book. My team has been with me for quite a while now, and I can't thank them enough.

My editor, Rich Baker, keeps me honest and never misses a chance to make me feel foolish. Ben Howard (www.eqco.one) has designed all of my book jackets, and he does a hell of a job. And he never complains. (I don't know how that's possible.) Danny Speight and DCO Publishing handle the eBook sales. I'm glad he does, as I don't have a clue how that works.

My beautiful wife Wassana keeps the wolves from the door and makes sure I always have a hearty breakfast (the most important meal of the day).

Finally, a great debt of gratitude to my publisher (and best friend) Boyd Willat. The first book was published by Asia Books, but from that point on Willat Publishing has carried the torch, including the new edition of *The Vampire of Siam* #1. I miss you Boyd. It's time we went on the road again.

To my readers, I suspect we'll be returning to Provence soon, and continuing the tale.

Jim Newport
Phuket, Thailand
2020

ABOUT THE AUTHOR

Jim Newport is a writer and Emmy-nominated production designer of both film and television. His film credits include *Bangkok Dangerous*, *Brokedown Palace*, *The Stepfather* and *Heart Like A Wheel*. In television he has set the "look" for many series by designing the pilot episodes of *The Lyon's Den*, *The Shield*, *The Education Of Max Bickford* and *China Beach*. His work on *The Piano Lesson* for the Hallmark Hall Of Fame was nominated for an Emmy in art direction. He was the production designer of season four of the worldwide hit TV series *Lost*. When not writing books or designing films, Newport performs as his alter-ego Jimmy Fame—a blues shouter, known to haunt the saloons and annual Blues Festival of his adopted home, Phuket, Thailand.

Please visit the author's website: www.vampireofsiam.com.

THE VAMPIRE OF SIAM SERIES

> *"These books are rich in cinematic imagery… and fascinating details of Thai history."*

— THAILAND TATLER

The Vampire of Siam series is an epic tale that spans half the globe and a course of 150 years.

In *The Vampire of Siam* (Book 1) a nineteenth-century explorer, Ramonne Delacroix, encounters an ancient Chinese demon in the temples of Angkor Wat. His subsequent nocturnal transformation leads him to the capital of Siam, where he witnesses the coronation of kings and the city's metamorphosis into the modern day sin-city of Bangkok.

Living the life of the lone hunter for the first 145 years of his incarnation as a night stalker, the vampire is reborn in *Ramonne* (Book 2) and eventually seeks to know the true extent of his powers. As he learns, he evolves. By the second book's end, the vampire's strength is enormous and he has control of the true magic he has been vested with.

In *The Reckoning* (Book 3) Ramonne, armed with newfound knowledge, seeks the source of his powers. He journeys back to Cambodia and the ancient temples to a fateful encounter with Zhoupeng—the mighty devil who "turned him" so many years before. Ramonne vows to put an end to Zhoupeng's reign of evil over the poor land.

Throughout the three books, Ramonne's fate is inextricably entwined with that of Martin Larue—wealthy American expat. Drawn to each other by mutual admiration and fascination, they eventually end up relying on each other to sort out the twisted path they find themselves thrust upon.

Together they face vampire-hunters, corrupt cops, opium dens, bordellos, blind fortune-tellers, jealous lovers, terrorists, suicide-bombers, smugglers, warlords and soul-sucking demons.

The Siamese Connection (Book 4) begins in 1948 Bangkok, shortly after the end of WWII and the Japanese occupation of Siam. The vampire, Ramonne Delacroix becomes involved in a quest for a mysterious artifact—The Oracle—hidden during the war by the Japanese. He joins forces with the famous American Expat Jim Thompson, (before he was the Silk King he was an OSS agent) and together they do battle with the nefarious Japanese Black Dragons.

The tale continues in the present day picking up where *The Reckoning* left off. Martin Larue and his pregnant wife Areeya cross paths again with the vampire and soon they too are involved in a deadly game of cat and mouse with the descendants of the Black Dragons, who are still in search of the mysterious Oracle.

A fast-paced blend of fact and fiction, *The Siamese Connection* finally solves the mysterious disappearance of Jim Thompson.

"Newport artfully shapes the vampire legend into a Mekong cocktail of surprises." Christopher G. Moore.

CHASING JIMI

Chasing Jimi is a rock 'n' roll period piece. It spans one year - the summer of 1966 to the summer of 1967. From New York's Greenwich Village to swinging London to the stage of the Monterey Pop Festival. It follows the ascension of one Jimmy James, a struggling back-up guitar player, to the exalted throne of rock-god superstardom.

On the road through merry-old England with the re-named Jimi Hendrix we meet the madcap royalty of the British pop scene. Jimi forms an endearing friendship with Rolling Stones founding member Brian Jones, whose battles with numerous personal demons and plunge from the top mirror Jimi's rise and fascination with the drug culture.

As the Jimi Hendrix Experience gains recognition, Jimi's past associations throw their own stumbling blocks in his path. Contracts signed by him as a hungry studio session musician surface. Jimi's management team are able to put out most of these fires, but one particularly sleazy New York record producer refuses to be bought out, and even goes so far as to send a couple of Brooklyn wiseguys to London to bring back his artist.

Chasing Jimi is "The Sopranos" meets The Beatles. The author's intense admiration for Jimi Hendrix, his own magical experiences as a hippy in the great Summer of Love and a stint as a touring rock 'n' roll photographer in the 70s served as inspiration for Chasing Jimi.

Knowing the scrutiny he would be under for daring to write a fictional piece about Jimi, the author strived to be as accurate as possible in the timeframe of events. Liberties were taken, but they were taken in order to craft what hopefully is an amusing and entertaining tale that transports the reader back to a better time.

"Did you miss the 1960s? This funny, yet loving and respectful adventure mystery about the decade's electric sugar stud will take you back."

— JERRY HOPKINS, AUTHOR OF *THE DOORS:*
NO ONE HERE GETS OUT ALIVE.

TINSEL TOWN: ANOTHER ROTTEN
DAY IN PARADISE

"Tinsel Town is the best introduction-to-Hollywood novel I've ever read."

— DAVID GILER, PRODUCER/WRITER *ALIEN,
UNDISPUTED, MYRA BRECKINRIDGE* AND
MANY MORE.

A Hollywood novel by an author who has been there - done that. Jim Newport is an Emmy-nominated production designer of both film and television. His experiences in the early years of his career served as the inspiration for Tinsel Town.

Memoirs from those in the film trade are nothing new. The bookshelves are crowded with star biographies—directors, writers and producers offering to show how difficult and arduous it is to either direct, write or produce a movie. But Tinsel Town is no simple straightforward autobiography. Like Chasing Jimi, it is a work of 'faction' - combining fact and fiction. Tinsel Town doesn't gloss over the cracks in the scenery —the grit, the stench, the plain old-fashioned blood and sweat that making movies was really about in the wild and woolly Easy Rider days of independent filmmaking. A non-stop party.

Art student Joey Morton arrives in Hollywood in 1968 and stumbles onto a sound stage. It was everything a young New Yorker could possibly hope to find—sex, drugs, gorgeous women, backstage passes, access to movie stars, rock 'n' roll… and more sex and drugs.

The author not only gives the reader a glimpse into what it

was like to enter this privileged profession in arguably its most exciting time (when movies played out in front of your own star-struck eyes, rather than against a green screen to be digitally composited later), but he also spins a tale, unravels a mystery, and takes the reader on an adventure.

"Newport's novels succeed in their purpose ... they entertain."

— THE NATION.

"It moves like a runaway asteroid." Tim Hallinan, bestselling author of the Poke Rafferty series (set in Bangkok).

— TIM HALLINAN, BESTSELLING AUTHOR OF
THE POKE RAFFERTY SERIES (SET IN
BANGKOK).